STIFF COMPETITION

Mr. Kluklinski ignored Mr. Walsh's hand. "Unfortunately, we don't have time for friendly."

He turned to confer with a young man and the same young woman he'd so recently shouted at.

Quietly, Brandon said to the girl, "He wears his underwear a little tight, doesn't he?"

"We can't help being nervous. Finals are coming right up."

"Finals? What is this, the Big Time?"

"Trisha," Mr. Kluklinski shouted, "did you come to skate or to talk?"

"See you," Trisha said. She smiled as she skated onto the ice.

Brandon was fascinated by Trisha. It was rare that a girl could give him any kind of competition in sports, and it never happened on the ice. Also, he'd never before met a girl who had an entourage. "Wait a second," he called to her. "When do I get a rematch?"

"I'm on the ice by five-thirty."

"In the morning?"

But she was no longer listening to him. She was skating slowly in a big circle, her eyes nearly closed, obviously in her own ice zone.

Don't miss these books in the exciting
BEVERLY HILLS, 90210 series

Beverly Hills, 90210

Beverly Hills, 90210—Exposed!

Beverly Hills, 90210—No Secrets

Beverly Hills, 90210—Which Way to the Beach?

Beverly Hills, 90210—Fantasies

Beverly Hills, 90210—'Tis the Season

And, coming soon

Beverly Hills, 90210—Where the Boys Are

Published by
HARPERPAPERBACKS

Based on the television series created by
Darren Star

SPELLING ENT. INC.

TWO HEARTS

A novelization by Mel Gilden based on a teleplay by
Carl Sautter and two teleplays by
Steve Wasserman & Jessica Klein

HarperPaperbacks
A Division of HarperCollinsPublishers

This is a work of fiction. The characters, incidents, and dialogues are products of the author's imagination and are not to be construed as real. Any resemblance to actual events or persons, living or dead, is entirely coincidental.

HarperPaperbacks   *A Division of* HarperCollins*Publishers*
10 East 53rd Street, New York, N.Y. 10022

Cover and insert photos by Andrew Semel and Timothy White

First printing: February 1993

Printed in the United States of America

HarperPaperbacks and colophon are trademarks of HarperCollins*Publishers*

❖ 10 9 8 7 6 5 4 3 2 1

Contents

1

The games people play

BRANDON WALSH SKATED IN LITTLE FIGURE eights while everybody waited for Steve Sanders, their goalie, to get back on his feet. He felt energetic and excited, jazzed by the game and eager to play some more. Deep inside his suit—under his padding, behind his mask—Brandon felt invulnerable. He was the ice man, and the other team better watch out when he cometh.

They were playing hockey inside a rink called the Ice Dome. Steve liked to call the place the Ice Doom, and sometimes the Ice Dumb, but that was only because ice skating was new to him and he kept falling down. Brandon himself was very comfortable on the ice, in the cold. The Ice Dome was a little bit of Minnesota set down here in Beverly Hills.

"This is nothing like roller skating, Walsh," Steve cried as he climbed to his feet.

"That's not what Wayne Gretzky told me," Brandon called back as he continued to circle.

Steve might get used to ice skating, but at the moment it was not his favorite thing in the world to do. Generally, he was fast on his feet and good with his mouth; looking like a klutz had to be a new experience for him. He was a handsome blond dude who did not react well when he found himself at the short end of anybody's stick.

As another player slid in his direction, Brandon smiled at the crazy things popular culture had done to them all. With hockey masks on, they each looked like Jason in *Friday the Thirteenth*. The player grabbed Brandon to stop himself.

"So, Dylan," Brandon said. "Do you love it? Are you hooked?"

Dylan shrugged. "It's not the ocean, but I could get used to the cold."

Dylan McKay was the boyfriend of Brandon's sister, Brenda, and a monster surfer. He was the cool dude that Steve wanted to be, and something of a man of mystery and romance at West Beverly High. Getting Dylan to admit he could become used to ice skating Brandon considered to be a major accomplishment.

Off the ice, Brandon was just one more school

kid buried near the middle of the bell curve. Being the best at something was an usual experience for him, so he allowed himself to enjoy it. He got in a couple more good shots before the coach blew his whistle and told them their time was up.

The coach was his father, which so far had not been a problem. They were both so into *the game,* forgetting outside connections was not only easy but unavoidable.

Brandon went to help Steve, who looked as if he would crawl off the ice on his hands and knees if that was the only way he could manage it. "Come on, bro," Brandon said. "Nice and easy."

"This ice hates me. I can tell," Steve said as he glided awkwardly toward the exit. "I do better with ice in cubes. You know, like in a glass with tea?"

He and Brandon stopped for a moment to watch the figure skaters glide onto the ice. They came in all shapes, sizes, and ages, from little kids who could barely walk to a very pretty dark-haired girl who came onto the ice leaping and spinning, giving Brandon the impression she had been released into her natural habitat. They all had two things in common: very short skirts and very white skates.

Brandon didn't even try to conceal his disgust. Those figure skaters were cream puffs compared to a guy who played hockey. Sure, figure skating took some practice, but the people who were skating against you were not out on the ice at the same time, trying to ruin your score. Made all the difference. Still, that dark-haired girl was very cute.

"Wow," said Steve. "Who is she?"

"The resident prima donna, I guess. Every rink has one. Whoa!"

The prima donna was skating toward them backward and as she brushed by them, knocked them down. They sprawled, spinning on the ice like pinwheels. Brandon was thinking in words he would never say out loud. Who did these fancy-dancy people think they were, anyway?

Then the girl came back with an expression of genuine concern on her face. Brandon was already getting to his feet, but Steve was still foundering around. As she helped him up, she said, "I am so sorry. It was all my fault."

"You can plow into me anytime," Steve said. He gave her the patented Sanders grin and Brandon was surprised the ice around her didn't melt. Steve still had hold of her hand. Brandon couldn't tell whether he really needed the support or not.

Maybe it was because his hormones were still pumping from the game, but Brandon wasn't ready to allow a pretty face to excuse rudeness. He said, "Don't you know that you're supposed to allow the *real* skaters time to get off before the charge of the ice brigade begins?"

The girl crossed her arms and looked at Brandon sarcastically. "I see," she said. "You mean *real* skaters as opposed to ice bunnies."

Brandon shrugged and said, "If the blade fits . . ." He allowed the rest of the aphorism to dissipate in the cold air, like the smoke of his breath. He was feeling very clever and powerful. Hockey was a great game, and playing it always left him high.

"Spoken like a true stickman. You know, medical studies show that a four-minute routine requires more stamina than a full period of hockey."

"Please," Brandon said, and waved her away.

He took hold of Steve, and as they once more started to skate toward the exit, the girl said, "Six laps around the rink. Just you and me."

Brandon swiveled slowly to look at her. From the steely glint in her eye he realized she wasn't kidding. He got Steve off the ice, and then stroked back to where she waited confidently. He considered going easy on her, but then decided she needed to be taught a lesson. She had to understand there was more to skating than scribing pretty patterns in the ice.

Jim Walsh organized himself into being referee. Brandon knew that wouldn't buy him anything even if he'd wanted it. Not only would he be completely fair, Jim Walsh might even give the girl an advantage just so nobody would accuse him of giving Brandon an advantage.

When his father gave the signal to start, Brandon was off like a shot. Then he hit his stride, and he stroked along easily, aware that six laps made a long race. He could hear the girl not far behind and to his right.

By the fifth lap, he was aware of exactly how long a six lap race could be. The shouting of the spectators had long since faded behind his labored breathing and his rapidly crumbling wall of concentration. He was losing his form and the girl was gaining on him.

He went into the sixth lap hoping that he would die before he had to finish it. Somebody had thrust a hot iron into his side, and he felt as if he was breathing through cardboard. Half a lap left, a quarter: he gave one last burst of speed as the girl came up exactly even with him.

That was the way they crossed the finish line. They skated slowly back to where Mr. Walsh waited with a quizzical expression on his face. He said, "A tie?"

Mr. Walsh's decision met with the approval of everyone in the stands. They went crazy with shouting and applauding.

Brandon leaned on the wall around the rink, and the girl joined him. She was barely even flushed. And unlike Brandon, she leaned against the wall because it was there, not because she had to. Against his will, he found his admiration for her increasing. And she was very cute.

When he could speak again, Brandon asked, "You let me tie, didn't you?"

"No way," the girl said pleasantly. "I'm much too competitive for that."

"What is going on here?" someone across the rink bellowed.

The girl seemed suddenly anxious. Even the atmosphere in the rink changed. It was as if a mountain lion had entered a forest full of rabbits and sparrows.

As the man who had shouted climbed down the bleacher stairs, Brandon stared at him. He was a big man wearing a long leather coat with a fur collar. He was nearly bald, and had big mustachios, like a circus strongman. Under his arm he carried a clipboard that seemed tiny in his grasp. He moved with confidence and some grace, like a man who was accustomed to being in charge and had no inhibitions about flaunting his authority.

Brandon wondered if it was really possible to deduce all that just from watching him walk down some stairs. Even Sherlock Holmes had his limitations.

The man stopped to gesticulate to a young woman dressed in a red, white, and blue warm-up suit. "This is what you do with world-class skaters when I'm not here to baby-sit?" The woman shook her head and tried to explain.

The guy would not let her. Whoever he was, he really thought a lot of himself. So far, Brandon was not impressed. The guy yelled to the girl, and she tried to smile. "Are you asking to get hurt? Is that what you want, Trisha?"

"No, Mister Kluklinski."

He walked up and back along the wall conducting the ice. "Look at the condition of the ice. Where's the Zamboni? Who is responsible for this mess?"

Mr. Walsh approached Mr. Kluklinski and put out his hand. "I'm sorry. It was just a little friendly competition."

Mr. Kluklinski ignored Mr. Walsh's hand. "Unfortunately, we don't have time for friendly."

He turned to confer with a young man and the same young woman he'd so recently shouted at.

Quietly, Brandon said to the girl, "He wears his underwear a little tight, doesn't he?"

"We can't help being nervous. Finals are coming right up."

"Finals? What is this, the Big Time?"

"Trisha," Mr. Kluklinski shouted, "did you come to skate or to talk?"

"See you," Trisha said. She smiled as she skated onto the ice.

Brandon was fascinated by Trisha. It was rare that a girl could give him any kind of competition in sports, and it had never happened on the ice. Also, he'd never before met a girl who had an entourage. "Wait a second," he called to her. "When do I get a rematch?"

"I'm on the ice by five-thirty."

"In the morning?"

But she was no longer listening to him. She was skating slowly in a big circle, her eyes nearly closed, obviously in her own ice zone.

"Let's get out of here," Steve said. "I think I have frost bite, and I want to go home and count my toes."

Brenda had really gotten into her work at Tracy Ross. After the craziness of the post-Christmas sales was over, the store had quieted down and

Diedre had time to show her something besides the most basic quick and dirty sales techniques. Diedre had even allowed her to take home a selection of Kathryn Enyart starter sets so that Brenda could practice on her mother.

They'd been at it for a few hours, ever since dinner. The timing was perfect. Brandon and her dad were out playing hockey at the local rink; the men would be neither underfoot nor available for comment. Now the kitchen table was covered with lipsticks, pots of eye shadow, compacts of powder, fanciful bottles of perfume, and jars of face cream.

Mrs. Walsh was resistant to trying anything new. Generally, with a little blush and a little lipstick she was ready to go. But Brenda was convinced that given half a chance, she could bring out a more romantic, more polished, more *glamorous* Cindy Walsh.

Mrs. Walsh watched herself warily in the mirror Brenda had set up on the kitchen table among the other paraphernalia. Using a soft brush, Brenda was applying another layer of powder to Mrs. Walsh's cheeks.

"Apricot Temptation," Brenda said. "Perfect for your coloring. That's the one."

"You think?" Mrs. Walsh asked. "I don't look like Madonna?"

"Depends on what Madonna looks like this week."

Brenda laughed along with her mother. A little laughter relaxed the customer, put them into a buying mood. Speaking of which, back to business. Brenda said, "I really think you should go with the raspberry cream."

"You don't think it's too bright?"

The raspberry *was* awfully bright. Brenda said. "No. It's actually sort of neutral. Don't you think?" Brenda hated hustling her mother this way, but it was nothing personal. It was business. Diedre said that most customers don't really know what they want till you tell them they want it.

Mrs. Walsh continued to study her reflection with some concern. She flashed occasional tentative smiles, which Brenda took as a good sign.

The kitchen door slammed open and Brandon and Mr. Walsh stomped in. They looked normal size, but each of them gave the impression that they took up a lot more space than usual. Suddenly, the kitchen seemed very small.

Brenda shook her head. With them around making smart comments, her mom might not buy anything. Men just didn't understand the art of makeup. They thought that Kim Bassinger looked like that right out of the shower.

Still studying her reflection in the mirror, Mrs. Walsh smiled and asked how practice went. She took a little more of the Apricot Temptation and considered the effect as she brushed it on.

While Brandon browsed noisily through the refrigerator, Mr. Walsh said, "It's been a long time since I showed anybody how to do a body check, but I have to tell you, it felt great."

Brandon emerged from the refrigerator with arms full of cold cuts and condiments. He made a little space for himself on the kitchen table and hunted for bread.

Brenda tried to stay calm. Eventually, they would leave. She would just wait them out. "Don't get mustard in the lip gloss, Brandon," Brenda said.

"Lip gloss?"

Mrs. Walsh said, "So, what do you think?"

Brandon was building his sandwich directly on the table instead of using a plate, which was gross. Crumbs were getting into the powder. Stay calm, Brenda told herself. This is good training in case I ever work at the zoo.

As Brandon slathered a slice of bread with mustard, (he used a knife instead of his finger, for which Brenda was grateful), he said, "If anyone can whip us into a team, Dad can."

"No. I meant me." She looked up at her husband and smiled without certainty.

For the first time, Mr. Walsh took a good look at his wife. Reluctantly, he answered, "Well, it's different."

Brandon held the sandwich in one hand, and with the other, picked up a tiny jar. "Apricot Temptation? What is all this?"

Be civil, Brenda reminded herself. "Just some samples I brought home from the boutique. We're giving Mom a kicky new West Coast look."

"As what? A clown?"

Mrs. Walsh looked up at Brandon and with sudden worry said, "Brandon, what did you do to your face?"

Brandon put down the Apricot Temptation and touched his cheek. He shrugged. "Part of the game."

"It's a nasty cut. Use iodine."

"Right, Mom. Go easy on her, Bren. G'night, Dad. Good game." Still clutching his sandwich, he left the kitchen and Brenda breathed a little easier.

Mrs. Walsh said, "Now I remember why I love hockey so much."

"It's just a scratch," Mr. Walsh said as he pawed through what Brandon had left of the sandwich makings.

"Let this be a lesson to you, Brenda. When men get a cold, they act as if they're dying. But when they bang into each other until they look like hamburger, they're having a wonderful time."

"It's the broken chromosome," Brenda said. "Same thing that makes them fans of the Three Stooges. So, which one of these cosmetics do you want to order?"

With some confusion, Mrs. Walsh looked at the array on the table. She said, "Let me sleep on it, okay, honey?"

"Okay. But I'm going to work early tomorrow."

"Don't worry. I'll be up."

This was bad, Brenda thought. Instinctively she knew that if she didn't make a sale tonight, when the sales pitch was fresh, Brenda might not sell anything at all. Only if she thought fast might she be able to salvage something of the evening.

"Good night, Mom. Tonight was a lot of fun."

Brenda was glad she hadn't lied about that. It had been fun. She and her mom didn't spend enough quality time together. Still, it would be nice if her mom bought something.

She went upstairs and found Brandon wincing as he dabbed iodine onto his cut. Men and their games. They were ridiculous. She stood at the bathroom door and watched for a moment before she went in to take off her makeup. She had quite a bit of it on. That's what happened when you tried to sell the stuff: you had to wear it.

"Deep gash," she said.

"Yeah," Brandon said. "The girl who ran over me is one terrific skater."

She couldn't have heard correctly. "You have a girl on your hockey team?"

"No, no." He put away the iodine and made faces at himself in the mirror. "She's just someone I met. Supposed to be some kind of Olympic hopeful. Her name's Trisha Kinney." He yawned and walked into his room.

She wouldn't allow Brandon to get away from her that easily. Brenda had actually heard of Trisha Kinney. She wasn't just another Olympic hopeful. She was nationally ranked. And not very far down, either. "I read about her in the *Times*. What's she like?"

"I don't know," Brandon said. He pulled off his shirt and tossed it into a corner. "Very competitive, of course." He smiled. "And kind of sweet. I'm going to ask her out."

"Have a good time."

"You don't think she'll go out with me?"

"Oh, she'd go out with you if she'd go out with anybody. But I hear that every moment of her life is planned, and that she's surrounded by nutritionists and trainers, and that if she does have a free minute, she studies so she can get her high school diploma."

"I'm a pretty adaptable kind of guy," Brandon said, and then he threw her out because he was going to bed.

2

No cream puff

THE NEXT MORNING, BRENDA WAS UP SO early she was certain she'd beat Brandon out the door, but by the time she made it to the bathroom he was already gone. She shook her head. Men and their hopeless romances.

Brenda dressed carefully. Then she took a lot of time with her hair and makeup—even more time than she might take for an important date. Most guys didn't really care about the finer points of grooming as long as you wore something tight, short, or transparent—preferably all three. Diedre would not be so forgiving. For her, image was everything. They were meeting for breakfast at Enyart's Patisserie, and she was certain that Diedre would not dress in jeans and a T-shirt just because it was Saturday.

Brenda found Mom in the kitchen drinking coffee while she read the paper. She glanced at Brenda with raised eyebrows.

"I'm having a power breakfast with Diedre. She's teaching me everything she knows about the business. She said that some day I would be a star." Brenda could not help being excited just thinking about it. In her head, she was already decorating that trendy little Rodeo boutique called Brenda Walsh.

"Of course you'll be a star," Mrs. Walsh said. "Retail is in your blood."

"Mother, please." Brenda didn't know whether to be horrified or encouraged.

"It's true. Your grandfather once owned the biggest furniture store in St. Paul."

"A boutique on Rodeo is not really the same thing."

"Nonsense. Retail sales is retail sales."

This discussion was getting out of hand. If Brenda didn't hurry, she'd be late. "Speaking of sales, have you decided which cosmetic you'd like to buy?"

Mrs. Walsh's expression reminded Brenda of a deer caught in headlights. Then Mrs. Walsh chose one of the smaller items—the Apricot Temptation Blusher—and wrote out a check. Brenda knew that

Diedre wouldn't be happy, but short of buying the stuff herself, there was no way to make a bigger sale.

Enyart's Patisserie was on Robertson in the gallery district. Diedre was already sitting at a sidewalk table with a half-eaten bran muffin and a cup of espresso in front of her. As usual, she looked terrific. Brenda hoped she could measure up.

Brenda ordered a bran muffin and an espresso—though she knew the caffeine would make her vibrate all day—and showed the twenty-dollar check to Diedre.

Diedre was disgusted, but she also understood that a woman like Mrs. Walsh could be a tough sale. Not only that, but she had an approach that Brenda immediately saw would be useful. "You've got to restore their consumer confidence," Diedre said. "You know, tell them that quality endures. You get what you pay for. Yada yada."

"I remember. We're not selling cosmetics and clothing. We're selling self-image."

"Exactly. You have about three seconds to size up a customer. What makes this one tick?"

Brenda shook her head. "There's so much to learn. You really think I have a talent for retail?"

"Tracy Ross is not a charitable institution," Diedre said. "I don't hire cream puffs." She sipped her espresso.

Brenda nodded. She knew she was no cream puff. A few hours later, she was in Tracy Ross trying to prove it. She hovered around Donna Martin and

Kelly Taylor, who had been pawing the merchandise for almost an hour. At the moment, Donna was pondering the perfume. She was actually about to buy something until Kelly sniffed the stuff on Donna's wrist and said, "It's okay if you want to smell like a luau."

Brenda looked across the room at Diedre, who was holding an arm full of blouses, skirts, and scarfs for a middle-aged woman wearing a flower print dress. Diedre would make a small fortune on that commission alone. And here was Brenda, stuck with these two deadbeats. "Come on, you guys. There must be something here you like."

They sampled perfume for a few more minutes, and then Donna found another one that made her smile. Kelly actually judged it "acceptable," or at least not actively offensive.

"Great," said Brenda with some relief. "Cash or charge?"

"How much is it?" Kelly asked. She looked for a price tag on the tiny golden bottle. "A hundred and ninety dollars," she said with alarm.

Donna's eyes got big. Evidently, two hundred bucks for a half ounce of smelly water was a little steep even for her. But Brenda was no cream puff. She said, "You're buying self-image." Unfortunately her statement came out sounding more like a question.

Kelly took the perfume bottle away from Donna and set it firmly on a table with a lot of other tiny bottles. "So," asked Kelly, "when do you get lunch?"

Brenda didn't want lunch. She wanted sales. She wanted commissions. She wanted to be a star!

Early that morning, long before Brenda had carefully chosen her wardrobe or even stumbled to the bathroom, Brandon had been awakened by his alarm. He groaned and lay back in his bed wondering if getting to know Trisha Kinney better was worth the effort of rising from this bed.

"It is. It is," he mumbled to himself as he threw back the covers. By the time he finished his shower, he was feeling almost human. He took an apple from the kitchen fruit bowl and went out into the crisp morning air. The house next door was just a big shadow. He stood on the step for a moment and enjoyed breathing the cleanest air Los Angeles would have that day. Very high, a jet went over.

He ate the apple while he drove his Mustang through the nearly empty streets to the rink. He felt a kinship with the other drivers. They were all on important business. Nobody would be up this early if they were not.

By the time he reached the rink, golden light was washing the eastern sky. He stuck the apple core into his car's ashtray, got out, and locked the door. At this hour, doing small things properly was important. As he walked to the double glass doors, he saw a light on inside the rink. To his surprise, the doors were not locked.

Inside, Brandon got himself some coffee from a

machine and took a sip. The stuff in the cardboard cup did not taste like coffee, exactly, but at least it was hot. He strolled into the main arena and saw Trisha doing stretching exercises on the floor at the side of the rink.

"So," said Brandon, and Trisha looked up at him. When she saw who it was, she smiled and Brandon felt good all over. He had just about convinced himself that he was the guy who could make her happy. But was there room in her life for both Brandon Walsh *and* ice skating? He said, "Is this the glamorous life of an ice queen?"

She stood and walked toward him. She was small and lithe. Brandon wasn't such a goof to still believe that hockey players were better than figure skaters. Different, maybe, but not better. Still, he found it difficult to believe that a person who appeared to be so fragile had the strength and stamina to be a competitive ice skater.

She stood next to him, and together they stared out at the ice as if it were the Pacific. She said, "This is by far the best part of the day. It's the only time when I feel my life is my own." She frowned.

For all the people around her, Brandon realized that this was one lonely little girl. He asked, "What's the matter?"

After a moment, she said, "Sometimes the pressure gets to me, that's all."

"I can imagine. But I know what you need."

She smiled suddenly. "A triple axle?"

Brandon was entirely at a loss.

"Sorry," Trisha said. "That's a little skating humor."

"Very humorous. But actually, I was thinking you needed a date with a hockey player."

"Sounds great. But I don't think Mister Kluklinski would go for it."

"We could always ask him."

"It doesn't work that way."

They heard voices, and looked up to where a group of young men and women were entering from the lobby. Some of them carried cardboard cups of coffee like the one turning cold in Brandon's hand.

"Quiet time is over," Trisha said. "But you can stay and watch me practice if you want."

"I can't think of anything I'd rather do." He grinned. "Well, I can, but . . ."

They both laughed. Then Trisha went to put on her skates. When she slid out onto the ice, she stopped being some cute girl to flirt with. She became a bundle of talent and hope and training, a symbol of grace under pressure.

And there was plenty of pressure. Coach K never let up on her. And while Brandon would not say that Trisha thrived on that constant mix of encouragement and criticism, she also did not buckle under it. He was impressed.

While he watched, Sal, the Zamboni man, sidled up to Brandon and asked if he was delivering a vending machine. Sal was a small muscular man who could have been brother to Nat down at the Peach Pit. Brandon responded stiffly because he guessed that Sal had been sent up here to throw him out, but it turned out that Sal was a big fan of Trisha's and he believed that she needed some real friends.

"You a real friend, kid?" Sal asked.

"I'm doing my best," Brandon said, and smiled.

Sal and Brandon watched together for a while. Then Sal said, "Fire and ice. What a skater," and went about his business.

Trisha smiled up at Brandon every so often, and then Brandon noticed that Coach K was taking an interest in him, too. Brandon figured he was in trouble, but he stood his ground. Trisha had invited him to watch the practice; he figured that no one but Trisha could make him leave.

Brandon was hypnotized by Trisha. She made the impossible things she did seem so simple. He was surprised when someone near him said, "Trisha has the potential to be a world-class athlete."

Brandon turned to see Coach K standing next to him. The coach was relaxed, and spoke in a conversational tone, but Brandon was suspicious. He knew that the coach hadn't come up here to ask his opinion on the jump Trisha had just made.

Coach K went on in the same quiet voice. "But in many ways, Trisha is a naive little girl who needs to focus on her skating—without distractions." He looked at Brandon, one eyebrow raised.

"Are you asking me to leave, Coach?"

"I am suggesting that if you left, it would be in Trisha's best interest."

Brandon considered that. On the one hand, Brandon was flattered to think that his presence might be a distraction. And yet, was it really fair of him to jiggle her elbow while she was doing the one thing in the world that was most important to her? Did she want her elbow jiggled? Did *she* really want the Big Time? Brandon decided he couldn't answer that question. Nobody but Trisha could answer it.

He said, "Maybe it's time to ask Trisha what she wants."

Coach Kluklinski looked at Brandon speculatively, one eyebrow up. He said, "Perhaps it is. But we cannot ask her now, while she is working. As a personal favor to me, and to her, I ask you to assume for this single occasion that what she has worked so hard for all these years is something she wants."

Put that way, the coach's request did not seem unreasonable.

"I'll go," said Brandon. "But I'll be back."

"I am certain of it, young man," Coach K said. "After all, you have a question to ask Trisha."

Brandon did not like the coach's confidence. It made him feel awkward as he climbed the bleachers to the aisle that circled the top of the rink. The awkwardness remained with him in the parking lot, and even on the drive home.

3

"I could have been a contender"

BRANDON WORKED ALL DAY AT THE PEACH Pit. During odd moments, he still felt awkward, and he wondered if he had been right taking such a strong stand against Coach Kluklinski. The expression on his face was impossible for Brandon to forget.

Not only was Brandon's brain full of questions, but getting up at five o'clock in the morning made for a very long day, especially because business at the Peach Pit had been brisk. His body felt like a sack of cement.

When he got home, Dad's car was not there and Brandon remembered that his parents had gone out to some kind of business dinner. But a light was on in the kitchen, and inside, Brandon found Brenda sitting at the table. She was wearing her comfiest cotton nightgown and eating ice cream from a big bowl. There were three scoops in the bowl, and Brenda had obviously been eating for a while. This could mean only one thing.

Brandon asked, "Hard day at the office?"

"You got that right," Brenda said. "I was on my feet for eight hours and probably made about a buck ninety-five in commissions."

"So much for heredity. Mom says Grandpa was a natural-born salesman."

Brenda sucked a hump of ice cream off her spoon and said, "You can do only so much with talent, Brandon. I'm beginning to think that our parents didn't prepare us for the real world. I think they blew it by raising us to be so . . ." Brenda searched for a good word.

"Nice?" Brandon asked.

"Exactly. Have some ice cream."

Brandon saw that it was almond crunch. Brenda knew how to pick ice cream, anyway. While he got a bowl and a spoon, Brandon thought about the opportunities he'd lost because he'd been too nice, because he hadn't been tenacious enough or competitive enough. He scooped ice cream into his bowl. Four scoops? Why not? Why not finish the whole half gallon?

"I could have been a contender," Brandon said. "I could have been somebody."

"Didn't Marlon Brando say that in a movie?"

"Right. *On the Waterfront.* You've been going to that revival house with Dylan again. But I'm the same. I was a pretty fair ice skater when I was a kid. How far do you think I could have gone with a little formal training? A little encouragement from the parents?"

"Absolutely."

Absolutely. Confidence gathered inside Brandon. He felt great, high on life. He and Brenda were young. They could still make up for the time they'd lost being nice.

"I am Walsh, hear me roar," Brenda said. "I can do anything."

"It's a competitive world. We need a competitive edge."

"And a killer instinct."

"And another half gallon of almond crunch ice cream."

With her mouth full, Brenda nodded. She swallowed and said, "Go for it, bro."

Brandon got a second half gallon of almond crunch from the freezer. He wouldn't let Coach K push him around. If Brandon wanted to watch her practice, that was between him and Trisha. He made up his mind to go back to the rink the first chance he had.

The next evening, Brenda felt a lot better about herself and her life. She was sitting at a table in the Peach Pit with a bunch of her friends—the usual suspects. Across from her were David Silver and Donna, at last out of the closet about their feelings for each other.

Brenda knew that in one of his pockets David carried a small white box tied with gold ribbon. She'd tied the ribbon herself. She'd sold him what was inside the small white box—the perfect gift for Donna, something really special. Brenda felt a sense of accomplishment knowing that she had the power to sell somebody something they hadn't even known they wanted. Retail sales was the final frontier, and she was its leanest, meanest inhabitant.

Like a magician, David put the small white box on the table in front of Donna. She seemed surprised and pleased, but Brenda's other friends were skeptical. David said, "You said everybody forgets your birthday because it's the same day as Christmas. Well, I wanted to show you I'm not everybody. I don't forget."

"Oh, David," Donna said.

"Are you going to open it," Steve asked, "or just admire the packaging?"

Donna carefully pulled off the ribbon, and then removed the cover. Inside, on a bed of cotton, was a bottle of the two-hundred-dollar perfume Kelly and Donna had rejected as too expensive the day before. Brenda could not contain her pleasure at having sold it to David, though the first effect on Donna was not all that she had hoped for.

Without touching it, Donna looked at the bottle. "It's so expensive."

"You're worth it," David said, and nodded to Brenda.

Brenda nodded back. This was great! Yes! She was the biggest, hairiest salesperson in the Rodeo Drive jungle.

Kelly leaned at Brenda and said, "How could you sell him something that expensive?" She sounded outraged.

"Excuse me," Brenda said. "But I didn't put a gun to his head. Besides, the customers do seem to be satisfied."

Donna had picked up the bottle and was cradling it like a small bird. She and David nuzzled. Brenda could almost hear the sexual energy buzzing.

Kelly said, "Donna's in shock, trust me. We'll see what happens when she and David come to their senses."

Brenda found it amazing that Kelly was so jealous of her job, her career. Yet, what else could be happening? She was about to talk to Kelly about it when the door opened and Brandon came in leading a really cute dark-haired girl.

She turned out to be Trisha Kinney, the famous ice skater. Brandon introduced her to everybody, proud as if he'd invented her.

Brandon hadn't planned to bring Trisha to the Peach Pit. He'd had enough trouble convincing Coach Kluklinski that he could get her home in one piece. Trisha had finally convinced the coach that Brandon was harmless, and he'd reluctantly allowed them to leave together. Brandon felt philosophical about being described that way; if he had to be harmless to drive Trisha home, so be it.

Actually, visiting the Peach Pit had been Trisha's idea. She'd asked him, "If you weren't driving me home, where would you be going?"

That seemed like an opening to Brandon, and he took it. Brandon wanted his friends to meet Trisha anyway, and he was right in guessing that the best place to find most of them would be the Peach Pit. Coach K might be angry that Trisha was not home in the hour Brandon had promised, but he couldn't be angry at Brandon. He could, of course, but it wouldn't be reasonable.

As they crossed Santa Monica Boulevard, Brandon said, "What is it with the coach? He acts like he's your father."

"In some ways he is," Trisha said. "There aren't many coaches in Fort Worth, so when he offered to take me on, I moved in with him and his wife."

"What about your real family?"

"Mom visits when she can. But I have sisters, and everybody's already made enough sacrifices for my career."

"Like what?" He stopped for a red light and looked at her. She seemed a little nervous. To a kid like Trisha, going to the Peach Pit must seem like an act of open rebellion.

"Trips to the rink at six every morning," Trisha said, "traveling to competitions, new boots every month, coaching, medical bills, convincing me to stay with it—"

"You wanted to quit?" Brandon interrupted with astonishment.

Trisha smiled wistfully. "At least twice a day.

What a life, Brandon thought. He said, "But it must be worth all the trouble. I look at how motivated you are and how much you've accomplished, and I feel as if I've been wasting the best years of my life."

At the green light, Brandon watched the road again.

"How can you say that?" Trisha asked. "At least you have a normal life. I've never had a date or gone to a real high school. I eat when and what I'm told. And a lot of people are depending on me and my career. I'm under a lot of pressure."

Brandon nodded. "Team Trisha."

Now, at the Peach Pit, Trisha studied Steve for a moment and said, "You know, you're much taller when you're standing up."

"Thanks, I think."

They all laughed.

"What's that wonderful smell?" Trisha asked.

Brandon put an arm around her shoulder and said, "That, my dear, is grease. It comes in many forms: burgers, fries, doughnuts. Doughnuts also contain sugar, of course, another one of the basic food groups. A strong America needs grease and sugar."

"And jojoba," Steve said.

"Right," said Kelly. "I wouldn't wash my hair without it."

"Nat makes the best grease burgers in the city, Trish. If you want one with the works, it'll be on the house."

Trisha shook her head. "Coach K would have a spinning tizzy. And it would throw my training table off balance for weeks. But thanks for the offer. When I want to be led astray, I know where to come."

"Pull up a chair anyway," Steve said. "Have a nice glass of water."

"I really have to get home."

"We promised Coach K," Brandon said, though he had difficulty believing having a glass of water with his friends would be a tragedy for Trisha's career. "The sectionals are in two days."

Everybody wished her luck.

"Or do we say, 'break a leg,' like in acting?" Donna asked.

Donna's question appeared to make the rest of them uncomfortable. Trisha defused the situation by saying, "Let's not and say we did. Oh, and if you're not doing anything on Saturday, I'd love to have all of you come as my guests."

Trisha's invitation was met with enthusiasm. Mindful of the time, Brandon ushered her out of the Peach Pit. They were followed by Brenda, who called after them, "Trisha, the store where I work sells the cutest leotards in the known universe. If you'd like, I can send some over to the rink."

Trisha's interest was no warmer than polite, but Brenda took that for encouragement.

This was not the Brenda that Brandon knew and loved. The old Brenda had been more concerned about people than about money. She would have been horrified to force leotards or anything else on her friends. If this was the new Brenda, the one with the killer instinct, Brandon would take almond crunch.

On Saturday, Brandon sat in the bleachers of the rink with Donna, David, Steve, and Kelly. As she had since that night at the Peach Pit, Donna smelled like the perfume David had given her. It was a pleasantly sexy smell, but Brandon was getting tired of it. Even the odor of cinnamon buns would get old after a while if it was not alternated with the odor of pizza. He thought of suggesting to Donna that if she wore the expensive perfume every day, she wouldn't have any left for really important occasions, but then decided not to bother. A woman who wore two-hundred-dollar perfume could make her own decisions.

Down on the ice, Trisha was doing pretty well, but only pretty well. In the last few days, Brandon had developed an eye for the fine points of competitive skating, and he knew that Trisha was losing points here and there. Worse yet, he knew that Trisha knew it. Certainly, nothing could undermine her confidence like knowing she wasn't doing her best.

Dylan sat down next to Brandon, and Brandon asked, "Where's Brenda?"

"She thought it would be an important career move to help Diedre take inventory."

"I see," Kelly said knowingly. Brandon had not been the only one to observe that Brenda was acting different lately.

"How's Trish doing?" Dylan asked.

Why not change the subject? If Brenda wanted to lose all her friends while she clawed out a career in retail, that had to be up to her. Skating, retail—ultimately what difference did it make? Still, Brandon could not let her go without taking the first chance he got to tell her how he felt.

"She's not doing so good in the short program," Steve said.

Brandon said, "Yeah, but this is do-or-die time. If she lands the double axle, she can still pull it out."

Trisha built up speed, leaped into the air, and Brandon was on his feet with his friends shouting, "Yes!"

Trisha hit the ground awkwardly and hard. Her foot twisted out from under her and she fell to the ice.

As Brandon watched in horror, all he could think about was Donna's innocent and unthinking wish that Trisha break her leg.

4

Distractions

BRANDON STOOD AT THE DOOR OF THE
warm-up room watching Coach Kluklinski attempt to
comfort Trisha. Every line in Trisha's body told
Brandon that she was unhappy. She and the coach
were sitting on a padded bench at the far end of the
room. In the short time Brandon had known him, he'd
been surprised to discover that—despite his rigorous
and unforgiving approach to skating—Coach K was
not without his soft side.

Brandon felt as awful as Trisha looked because
he was certain that her failure was his fault. His
hanging around had distracted her, just as the coach

had warned. If Brandon hadn't been so stubborn, Trisha would be out there taking victory laps instead of in here on the edge of tears.

"I just couldn't feel the ice," Trisha said.

"Every skater is entitled to a bad day."

Trisha sniffed. "What about the finals?"

Coach K put his arm around her and said, "You came in fifth, honey. I'm sorry, but for you this year's season is over."

"That's it?" Obviously, the judgment was even worse than Trisha had expected.

"Maybe you should think about going back to Texas for a while. Spend some time with your parents. Decide if you want to gear up for next year."

Brandon shifted his position and the coach glanced in his direction.

"I'll see you at home," the coach said. He nodded at Brandon as he went out.

Brandon walked to Trisha and sat on the spot Coach K had just vacated. Trisha didn't even look up.

"Tell me the truth, Trish. Is this my fault?"

She looked at him, and her expression broke his heart. He'd never seen anybody so entirely whipped. Still, she managed some surprise. "Your fault? How?"

"Coach K said I was distracting you."

"Listen, Brandon. It is no way your fault that I couldn't land a jump I haven't missed since I was twelve."

Brandon nodded, but he still didn't feel better.

Trisha sniffed again, and brought up an unconvincing smile. "The good news is that we can have that date now." She fell into his arms and cried.

Great. The consolation prize when you lose a trip to the Olympics was a date with Brandon Walsh. Third prize was two dates with Brandon Walsh. Sheesh.

Monday morning Brenda was in the kitchen making a last-ditch effort to sell cosmetics to her mom. Brenda didn't like making her pitch while her dad and Brandon were around—they continued to make rude remarks—but Brenda had no choice. The sale ended today, and if her mom wanted to save seventy-five dollars, she had to buy the whole Kathryn Enyart package this morning.

Brenda could see that Brandon disapproved of her applying eye makeup to their mom. She didn't know what was wrong with him. Maybe Diedre's predictions were coming true.

Sounding a little strained, even to herself, Brenda said, "I'm just trying to accent Mom's cheekbones to help her neutralize the age thing."

Mrs. Walsh looked at herself in the mirror critically.

Brenda tried to stay calm. But if her mom didn't buy something soon, she would be late for school as well as lose a sale. And then the phone rang.

Mr. Walsh put down his coffee cup and ran for the door. "If that's for me, I already left."

Mrs. Walsh put down the mirror and went to

answer the phone, leaving Brenda and Brandon alone in the kitchen.

Brenda said, "What is that dirty look you've been giving me all morning?"

"I'm just trying to figure out if I can stand being related to the new Brenda Walsh," Brandon said. "You know, the girl who'll say anything to make a sale?"

There it was. Diedre's worst fears were confirmed. "Look, Brandon, I'm sorry that everybody is so put off by the idea of an independent woman taking an aggressive posture in pursuit of a specific goal—which is to have my own car so I will no longer be at the mercy of my brother—but there it is."

"I see," Brandon said. He seemed amused. Why couldn't the big goof understand?

"Your friend Trisha knows what I'm talking about. Ask her if you don't believe me."

"Ask her yourself," Brandon said as he collected his books. "She's going to visit school today—beautiful exotic West Beverly High."

Maybe this conversation wouldn't be a total loss after all. Brenda said, "That's great. Did she happen to say anything about those leotards I sent over?"

"Not that I recall."

Diedre had been right about the male sarcasm, too. Brenda refused to react. But it would be a long drive to school.

Brandon began his date with Trisha by showing her around West Beverly High. His friends were astonished that anybody would come to school on purpose when they didn't have to, but Brandon had been correct about her finding it exotic. After all, she'd had nothing but private tutors all her life. Mass education was a real novelty.

They found Andrea Zuckerman in the *Blaze* office, and for a while, she and Trisha rattled on about ice skating. Evidently, Andrea had once wanted to be an ice skater. When she discovered that Trisha and Brandon were together on a date rather than an interview, Andrea's chattiness evaporated, though she did not go so far as to be impolite.

Brandon could see what was going on, and he tried to patch things up by inviting Andrea to lunch with them.

"No, thanks," Andrea said. "I have to stay here and, uh, grease the Linotype machine."

Brandon had never seen a Linotype machine outside a museum. Most papers set their type with computers, and the West Beverly *Blaze* did the same. But he wouldn't call her on her very thin excuse. Andrea had her reasons for not wanting to lunch with Brandon and a current squeeze, and Brandon would not question them. Jealousy was a drag.

Trisha sat in on Brandon's classes and was surprised to discover how much she knew. "Going to school is fun," she said.

"You get over it," Brandon assured her.

Later, Brandon and Trisha ran into Dylan, Steve, Kelly, and Donna on their way to lunch. Brandon said, "You are talking to a girl who has never eaten a Twinkie."

This caused a sensation. Donna offered to buy Trisha her first Twinkie.

"No no," said Kelly. "She must begin with vinegar and salt potato chips."

Steve rolled his eyes and recommended vast quantities of Ben and Jerry's ice cream.

"Dim sum from Chin Chin," Dylan said. "Cinnamon rolls from Nat's."

"Pizza from Anna's," said Kelly.

"Gum," said Donna.

Donna's suggestion caused some discussion whether gum was in fact a food. Trisha ended the discussion when she announced that she wanted to try it whether it was a food or not.

Brandon held up his hands and said, "Wait. I know a food that is told of in song and story. A food not found in nature. A meal so complete you eat the package. A food so cheap it is within reach of all those but the most abject. Nature's little joke on Julia Child. A food that keeps on giving hour after hour. After hour."

He refused to say more, but took them to the food truck that came daily to the student parking lot of West Beverly High. They waited while he ran over and made his purchase. He came back and presented it to Trisha with a flourish. "I give you," he said, *the burrito!*"

"What's inside it?" Trisha asked as she looked at it warily.

"Meat, cheese, guacamole, refried beans, many ingredients known only to the people who make burritos. Try it. You'll like it."

Trisha tried the burrito and smiled. Her life was now complete. The burrito disappeared in record time.

"None of my clothes will ever fit again," Trisha said happily.

"That reminds me," Dylan said. "Brenda asked me to ask you if you'd thought about those leotards she sent over."

"Sorry, no."

They all took a few moments to think about the new Brenda. And then Donna presented Trisha with her very first package of Twinkies. It was only after she'd eaten both cakes herself that it occurred to her that she should have shared them. Everybody assured her she had done the right thing.

"Greed is part of the Twinkie experience," Steve said.

That evening, Brandon was surprised when Trisha asked him to take her to the rink, but he did it anyway. After all, it was her first date ever and fantasies had to be indulged.

Trisha set a boom box on the lowest bleacher, and made Brandon put on skates while she put on her own. They stood at the edge of the ice enjoying the feeling of standing close together, enjoying the sight of the vast empty space lit only by soft red and green lights.

Trisha said, "I always wanted to go dancing on my first date."

"I don't dance."

"I know. But you do skate." She pushed a button on the boom box and a waltz began. Brandon wondered if it was "The Skater's Waltz." She pulled him onto the ice and they began to glide around it. They did nothing fancy, just made long graceful strokes, a slow turn, a fast burst on the straightaway.

The moment was magical. Brandon felt that he was flying. And he was certain that he was in love.

Brandon lost track of the time. Someone applauding from the sidelines awakened him as if from a dream. He and Trisha slid to a stop. They were both surprised to see Coach Kluklinski standing at the rail. Brandon resented the intrusion, but Trisha didn't seem to mind.

"Very nice," he said. "But you could use a triple axle and possibly a more contemporary piece of music."

Trisha smiled wearily. "I still haven't decided whether I want to continue with the program."

"I have some news that may influence your decision. This afternoon the Skating Federation granted a waiver for you to compete at sectionals."

Brandon saw how pleased this surprising news made Trisha. He was happy for her, of course, but he could not help guessing that he was about to lose a girlfriend.

"Is that possible?" Trisha asked.

"Anything the federation says is possible is possible. Maybe there were problems with the scoring. Maybe somebody appealed. Who knows? It's all politics. The important part of all this is that we have only five days to get ready. And because it is still early—"

"We have to start tonight?"

Coach K explained, "Everyone knows you're getting an exemption. The judges will be gunning for you."

Trisha considered that. Brandon was still standing at her side, but he might as well have been in another zip code. He felt as if she were going away, and maybe she was. Maybe she was already gone.

"We'll need to rechoreograph the program," Coach K said.

Trisha nodded. "Triple toe? Double loop?"

"That might work."

Brandon was just a civilian listening to two professionals discuss their craft. He had no idea how to leave gracefully. Perhaps if he just left, nobody would even notice.

Suddenly, Trisha turned to him and grabbed him by both arms. "Oh, Brandon. I'm so sorry."

"Sorry about what? That you have another chance to fulfill an ambition you've had all you're life? I'm real happy for you."

"Thanks, Brandon." She skated closer to Coach K, and they began to speak about skating again, discussing death spirals and lutzes, and other words Brandon had never heard before. He skated off the ice, exchanged his skates for his shoes, and walked up the stairs. Coach K cried suggestions to Trisha as she skated in big circles. Neither of them noticed when Brandon walked out the door.

Brenda decided that her mom had been right. She did have retail in her veins. Shortly after Diedre had gone to dinner, a woman slightly older than Brenda had come in and browsed through the store. She was slim and tan and good-looking in a standard TV way. She wore a T-shirt that said CARPE DIEM on it and tight jeans.

After fingering the necklaces for a while, she asked for Diedre.

Brenda sensed that this woman was ready to buy. And from the nonchalant attitude she showed toward the price tags, Brenda guessed that money would be no object. Brenda said, "Diedre's gone to dinner, but I'm sure I can help you find exactly what you're looking for."

The woman nodded.

Joyce—the woman's name was Joyce—went through the store stroking scarves, appraising jewelry, trying on clothes, and sniffing perfume. She liked the same perfume as Donna had, but put it in her growing pile of purchases without a second thought.

Joyce was such an easy customer, Brenda barely had a chance to try out the techniques Diedre had taught her over the past few weeks.

The next time Brenda looked at her watch, almost an hour had passed. But it had been a good hour, a great hour. She mentally calculated that the commission on this sale would almost make her week. It would run into the hundreds. Diedre would be really surprised when she came back.

By the time Diedre returned, Brenda was just taking an invoice from the box. On the counter next to her was a pile of clothes and accessories. Without exaggerating too much, Brenda estimated that Joyce was about to purchase one of everything in the store.

Brenda smiled at Diedre, but Diedre ignored her entirely. She and Joyce hugged, and talked about people Brenda had never heard of. Diedre seemed to notice the merchandise on the counter for the first time. She asked, "Did you get everything you need?" She joined Brenda behind the counter and picked up a few things to admire them.

"If I didn't, it's not Brenda's fault." She grinned at Brenda, and began to drift around the store again.

Brenda said, "I wouldn't recommend them to everybody, but see what you think of those blocky gold earrings."

Joyce held them in one hand for a moment, then tried them on. She studied herself in a mirror.

Diedre reached for the invoice that Brenda was about to fill out. This was such an unexpected move that at first Brenda didn't know what to make of it. But when Diedre actually began to write on it, Brenda whispered, "What are you doing?"

"Joyce has always been *my* customer."

"But if you ring up the sale, you get the commission." Brenda felt like an idiot stating the obvious, but what else could she say?

Diedre was writing fast now. She didn't even stop when she said, "Look, sweetie, this is real life. We're coming off the worst Christmas ever, business is not what it used to be, and I still have car payments to make. Get used to it."

Joyce wandered back with the big gold earrings and Diedre asked Brenda to get some boxes for all the stuff Joyce had just bought. All the stuff that Brenda had sold her. All the stuff that Diedre was about to ring up as her own. Brenda was hot, frustrated, and angry. Diedre had played her just like she played the customers. Brenda had to do something. But short of making a scene, all Brenda could do right now was get the boxes. She'd never felt so stupid.

5

Business as usual

BRANDON HAD NO TROUBLE GETTING UP AT five in the morning. The truth was, he hadn't slept much. He'd spent most of the night thinking about what it took to be a successful competitor in the real world.

He could have gone for the gold instead of having a normal life. But then he would have missed out on cinnamon rolls, ice cream, burritos, and even gum. Of course, he didn't remember anybody asking him what he'd wanted. His parents made the big decision. He didn't know whether or not he would have chosen differently than they did. Even sitting on his bed in the middle of a mild Beverly Hills night, he still didn't know. But he regretted not making the decision himself; he felt angry about it.

He wondered if Trisha had made her own decision. Hard to say. At first, she had seemed upset that she couldn't go to sectionals. But as far as Brandon could tell, she'd enjoyed her day at school, hanging out, eating all the junk she normally wasn't allowed. Of course, that had been only one day—maybe she just enjoyed the novelty. When Coach Kluklinski had announced that she could still compete, she'd climbed right back into her old straitjacket as if she'd never been away.

Brandon finally realized that he and Trisha would never be a couple—she was already going steady with the ice—but he could still be her friend. He could still support her in what she wanted to do. Maybe some day she'd be too old for figure skating. Who knew? People did get old.

He was on his way down the hall when his dad came out of the bedroom pulling on his robe. He thought nothing of the fact that Brandon was getting such an early start, but only reminded him that they had hockey practice that afternoon. Brandon had forgotten, but he promised he'd be there. He was still angry about not being given the opportunity to choose whether he wanted to be a world-class skater. Being half asleep, Mr. Walsh didn't seem to notice.

Brandon was puzzled by the number of cars in the rink's parking lot when he arrived at five-thirty.

This was usually Trisha's best time, the time she got to skate alone.

He heard voices arguing while he put money into the coffee machine. He hurried out onto the aisle at the top of the rink and saw Trisha skating in tiny figure eights while battles raged around her. No doubt, this was the rechoreographing Coach Kluklinski had talked about the night before. Brandon sat down to watch, though at the moment there wasn't much to see except a lot of passionate people waving their hands at each other and at the ice.

Sal, the old Zamboni guy, came at Brandon along the bleachers.

"Team Trisha back from the dead, eh, Sal?"

Sal seemed embarrassed. "Yeah, look, Brandon, no visitors allowed today. They're coming up with some new routines, and—"

"You tell Coach K for me—"

"This don't come from Coach K," Sal said. "It comes from Trisha."

Brandon was so surprised, that for a moment he thought he'd heard wrong. "Trisha?"

Sal nodded. "I'll have to ask you to leave."

Brandon felt betrayed. He looked down at Trisha, who was intent on the ice. Not even the arguments of her trainers had any effect on her. Maybe he hadn't been betrayed. Maybe he was just being told that there was no room in her life for skating and Brandon Walsh.

"Sure, Sal," Brandon said, and went back home.

It was a long few hours till hockey practice, and Brandon tried to use them constructively, but he could not keep his mind on his homework. Instead of seeing the books in front of him, he divided his time between feeling jealous of the ice, and feeling angry at his parents for denying him a chance at the big time. He could have been a great ice skater. He was sure of it.

He couldn't decide whether he was angry at Trisha. It would be unreasonable for him even to be disappointed. If that fluke fall hadn't happened, he never even would have had a date with her. Still, he would miss her. And he discovered that he was not only jealous of the ice, but of her success, the success he would never have.

By the time he went back to the rink, Team Trisha was no longer there. He would have been surprised if they had been there that late in the day. While still preoccupied with Trisha and thoughts about what he might be doing right now if he had lived up to his potential, he slowly put on his hockey gear.

Mr. Walsh and the hockey team arrived, and Brandon went out onto the ice. He kept missing shots; he even missed the puck entirely a couple of times. Steve, who actually managed to make a couple of saves, was playing better than he was.

Finally, Mr. Walsh called Brandon over and asked him what the problem was.

By this time Brandon was angry, but the anger was mostly directed at himself. He hated looking like a goof on the ice. He said, "No problem, Dad. I missed a setup. What's the big deal?"

Mr. Walsh studied him for a moment, and then he said gently, "Brandon, whatever happened with that girl this morning, it's not the end of the world. Is it?"

Was it? Brandon shrugged. He was just a kid. What did he know?

"She was something special, huh?" Mr. Walsh said.

"Let me put it this way, Dad: I didn't even try to kiss her."

"Wow," Mr. Walsh said appreciatively.

Brandon decided that as long as they were having a heart to heart, they might as well drag everything out into the open. Brandon said, "When I was a kid and I was winning all those trophies at the Y, how come you didn't encourage me to skate competitively?"

"We did encourage you. We just didn't push you."

"Didn't think I could handle the pressure?"

Mr. Walsh seemed shocked at the idea. He said, "Brandon, you didn't know this, but your mother actually met with one of the top coaches in the Midwest. He asked her one very important question. He wanted to know whether we wanted a superstar or a son."

Brandon was amazed that he had never before even considered the alternatives as a parent saw them. It had never occurred to him that his parents had made the decision they had because they wanted him, Brandon Walsh, and not some hot dogger they saw in person twice a year and the rest of the time on pay-per-view TV.

"I hope you're not disappointed by the choice we made."

"You did the right thing, Dad. Trust me."

They watched the rest of the team noodling around on the ice. Even Steve seemed to be getting his ice legs.

Mr. Walsh said, "So, you want to play another period?"

"No. I should get to work." He held out his massively gloved hand, and they shook awkwardly. Brandon, at any rate, felt better about his life. He supposed that made his dad feel more comfortable, too.

Brandon slid through his shift at the Peach Pit without thinking much about what he was doing. Of course, working at the Pit did not require heavy-duty brain activity so he was fine. Nat had to yell at him only once, when an order was up.

As it usually did, business tapered off about a half hour before closing. Brandon was wiping down the main counter—enjoying the zen of the work—when someone came up behind him and asked what was good. It was Trisha.

Except for TV, Brandon had not expected to see her again and so had not taken the trouble to decide how he would react. He found that he was stiff, nervous, and not very friendly. She had had a two-week fling and then dumped him. Nobody like to be dumped, not even if it was in favor of a lifelong obsession.

Brandon said, "If it doesn't contain grease or sugar it's not on the menu. I'm surprised you'd take a chance coming into a den of sin like this." He continued to make big circles on the counter with his rag.

Trisha remained calm. Nerves of steel, Brandon thought sarcastically.

She said, "Coach K and I are on our way to the airport, but I didn't want to leave without saying good-bye."

"Good-bye," Brandon said, then realized what a jerk he sounded like. "Look, you want a glass of water or something?"

"No. Thanks. Listen, Brandon, I had to close the practice today. I'm the one who wants to be the best skater in the world, not Coach K, or my parents or anybody else. Me."

"So, what was I? A two-week distraction?"

"I hope you don't think it's easy to give you up, Brandon. My life is full of tough choices." She smiled. "But you'll always be the guy who gave me my first burrito."

She kissed him lightly on the cheek, and then was gone. Brandon looked at the closed door for a long time before he went back to work. She would always be the girl who got him to dance.

*　　*　　*

Brenda heard her alarm go off, but she ignored it. She didn't think she'd ever get up again. In bed, she was safe and warm and did not have to compete with anybody. After what had happened between her and Diedre, she'd decided that having a killer instinct was a good deal only for the killer. Being the killee only made a person feel lost and alone and stupid.

Later, Mrs. Walsh came in and asked Brenda if she was ever going to get up. Brenda had work, after all, and among the Walshes such responsibilities were taken seriously.

At first, Brenda huddled into herself. She didn't want to talk about why she felt so bad. But Mrs. Walsh sounded so friendly and concerned that Brenda allowed herself to be jollied into a sitting position. Brenda explained what Diedre had done to her. "I wanted to quit yesterday, but you and Dad always make such a big deal about how winners never quit and quitters never win."

"Knowing when a situation is hopeless isn't quitting." Mrs. Walsh shook her head. "Your grandpa called people like Diedre barracudas."

"I was on my way to becoming a barracuda myself, wasn't I?"

"Well, you did go a little overboard."

"I tried to do what Grandpa said. I gave service with a smile—for all the good it did me."

"Grandpa said something else, too. He said, 'Don't get mad. Get even.'"

"That doesn't sound like Grandpa."

"That's because he was never mad at you." Mrs. Walsh nodded and smiled. The last time Brenda had seen her this way was when some woman had persisted in not paying Brenda for the baby-sitting she was doing. Mom had eventually taken the baby to the fancy event the woman was attending, and left it in her lap. The baby had not been hurt, but Brenda had never seen a woman so embarrassed. The woman never did pay Brenda, but the look of surprise on her face had been priceless.

"What are you going to do?" Brenda asked.

"When the going gets tough," Mrs. Walsh said, "the tough go shopping."

"What do you mean?"

"You just go to work, honey. And don't be surprised at whatever happens."

Mrs. Walsh wouldn't say any more, but Brenda felt encouraged enough to do as her mom suggested. Actually, Brenda had not been so excited about going to work since her first day at Tracy Ross.

When Brenda arrived, Diedre was already there dusting the merchandise. She was miffed that Brenda was late but couldn't dock her pay because Brenda theoretically worked on commission. Brenda said nothing about what had happened the day before, and neither did Diedre. Evidently, for Diedre, acting like a barracuda was business as usual. Brenda took pleasure knowing Diedre was about to get her reward, though she did not know what form that reward would take.

The morning was about average, except that every time somebody came in the door, Brenda looked over with anticipation, ready to back up whatever scheme her mother had in mind. And each time, Brenda was disappointed to see it was not her mother. While spending time with a big customer, Diedre actually allowed Brenda to make a few sales.

Diedre was in the middle of her wrinkle cream pitch when a tall woman, dressed to the teeth, entered the shop and peeked around over the top of her dark glasses. Her hair was wrapped in a turban of flimsy blue stuff; heavy bracelets dangled from her wrists, and her fingers were encrusted with rings that had ostentatiously large gems in them. She was perfect, the ultimate Beverly Hills customer, a Really Big Fish.

It was Brenda's mom.

When Diedre saw the Really Big Fish, she turned over the wrinkle cream pitch to Brenda and homed in. "Chanel is so classic," Diedre said as the Really Big Fish studied some jackets. "It would so complement—"

"I'll take this one," the Really Big Fish said, and handed a boldly patterned jacket to Diedre.

As highly as she thought of herself, Brenda was certain that Diedre was surprised at the ease of her sale.

"I'm bored," said the Really Big Fish. "I need some new things to liven up my wardrobe."

"You've come to the right place," Diedre said.

"We have some accessories over here that I think would be perfect for you."

Brenda sold the jar of wrinkle cream, and then enjoyed watching her mom and Diedre work out on each other. Diedre yammered about how perfect this was; and how the Really Big Fish deserved that; and how a belt was a little extreme, but the Really Big Fish could carry it off.

As Mom's purchases continued to pile up on the counter, Brenda became fearful. If she really intended to buy all this stuff, Dad would go through the roof. The pile already contained a few thousand dollars' worth of stuff. Besides, Brenda didn't see how buying out the store would teach Diedre a lesson.

Another thing that bothered Brenda was how convincing her mom was as a conspicuously consuming Beverly Hills matron. She'd completely fooled Diedre, and that wasn't easy. There was obviously a lot about Mrs. Walsh that Brenda didn't know.

Diedre sent Brenda into the back room to see if they had any scarves in teal, and when she came back, her mom was gone. With some trepidation, Brenda asked, "Where's Imelda Marcos?"

Excitedly, Diedre said, "She's outside feeding the meter. Have you been taking notes? This is the kind of lady you dream about. She knows what she wants and isn't afraid to shell out the big bucks; she has taste, but is not too discriminating." Diedre rubbed her hands together. "This may turn out to be a good year after all. Just watch me button this sale."

Brenda nodded, but said nothing. She didn't trust herself. Diedre had taught Brenda one useful skill, anyway, and that was how to read people. Brenda judged that Diedre was about ready for whatever Mrs. Walsh had in mind. Brenda couldn't wait.

Mrs. Walsh came back in with a parking ticket. "Too late. That's life." She didn't seem upset. As she thrust the ticket into her bag, Diedre offered to pay for it. Mrs. Walsh graciously let her. Only fair, Brenda decided. She hoped Diedre would have to pay for it out of her commission.

The Really Big Fish walked to her pile of potential purchases and pawed through them. She pulled out a garish pink belt with yellow lightning bolts on it and said, "You know, I'm not certain I need this belt."

"Of course not," Diedre said. "It's really not you." She took it from the Really Big Fish and hid it behind her back.

"And I'm wondering if I really need all these blouses," the Really Big Fish said, pondering.

Brenda noticed the wild look of dread in Diedre's eyes. But still holding firm, Diedre said, "You have such great taste. Just cull the ones you don't want, and I'll have the girl put them away."

The girl, Brenda thought. That was a hot one.

Brenda admired her mom more and more as the direction of this sale became obvious. She felt the satisfaction she always experienced when the bad guy was captured at the end of a movie. Watching the universe rocking back into balance warmed her soul.

"And I don't really need these scarves," the Really Big Fish said. "Or these shoes."

Diedre could no longer pretend that all was going as expected. "You don't?" she asked with some surprise.

"No," the Really Big Fish said angrily. She acted as if Diedre had been trying to cheat her for the past half hour. "No scarves, no shoes, no hundred-buck wrinkle cream. I really don't need you telling me how much you love my *good taste* and how *happy* this will make me and how much I *deserve* this, and how much I *deserve* that. Mostly, I don't need you kissing my butt to pad your commission while you treat your employees like dirt."

Yeah, Mom, Brenda thought while she stood innocently at Diedre's side. The shock on Diedre's face was wonderful. For the first time in Brenda's experience, Diedre was speechless.

"But thanks so much for taking care of the parking ticket. You *deserve* it."

Brenda watched Diedre watch her Really Big Fish stroll out of Tracy Ross without having bought so much as a button cover.

"Bitch," Diedre said.

"You got that right," Brenda said. "I quit."

"What?" Diedre asked. She was still in shock from having lost the sale of a lifetime.

"I've decided that retail sales is not for me. I'm not enough of a barracuda. Please send me my check." Using the gait her mother had so successfully used moments before, she strolled out of the store. Brenda wondered briefly if she would receive the money she'd earned. And then she decided she didn't care. Money was handy stuff, no doubt about it. But there were more important things.

Some evenings later, Brandon was watching the skating sectionals on TV. Brenda and Dylan were there too. Brandon would rather have been alone while he pined after Trisha, but he could hardly chase his sister and her main squeeze from the house, especially considering the main squeeze was one of his own best friends.

Trisha did good work. She landed the double axle like a champ, which she was. Brandon was delighted. Even missing her as he did, he could not help wishing her well.

After she triumphantly concluded her routine, a woman wearing earphones and carrying a microphone interviewed her. She said, "Congratulations, Trisha. Moments like these must make all the sacrifice and hard work worthwhile."

"Absolutely. Of course, I do miss the burritos." She smiled for the cameras, and it seemed to Brandon that she was smiling for him. It wasn't so bad to be remembered as the guy who fed Trisha Kinney her first burrito. Really.

Trisha had won the sectionals and lost burritos. Brandon still had burritos, but he couldn't help feeling he'd lost something he would miss even more.

Brandon didn't have much time to mope because the credits were still rolling on TV when his dad ran into the living room and announced excitedly, "It's here!"

6

The beat goes on

BRANDON KNEW WHAT "IT" WAS, BUT MR. Walsh refused to tell Brenda and Dylan. The only clue Mr. Walsh would give them was in the form of an invitation to the Peach Pit the next evening.

"I know what it is," Dylan said to Brenda. "Nat named a burger after your dad. Congratulations, Mister Walsh."

"Good guess, Dylan, but you're not even close. Come on, Brandon."

"See you guys later," Brandon said. He was glad to be distracted from thinking about Trisha. He could dream about her, but he doubted if he'd ever see her in person again.

Brandon climbed into the front seat of Mr. Walsh's huge dadmobile. When he rode shotgun with his father, Brandon always felt as if he were embedded in a wad of bubble gum. On the few occasions when he'd driven the car in traffic, he always felt as if he were maneuvering the starship *Enterprise* through an asteroid belt. There was almost enough room in the back seat to play nine holes of golf, and at the moment all of it was filled with cardboard boxes of various sizes. The biggest could hold a St. Bernard.

As he drove, Mr. Walsh sang under his breath, "Do wa diddy diddy dum diddy do." Brandon hoped that this was not a portent, but he was afraid his future contained a lot of singing.

The Peach Pit was closed, but Nat was waiting for them. He looked out from behind the shade, and Brandon had the urge to say, "Joe sent me." Nat saw who it was, and let them in.

The three of them worked hard carrying boxes in from the back seat. When they were done, they sat around a table. Nat studied the boxes as if they contained wild animals. "Are you sure about this, Jim?" he asked.

"You read the brochures my clients sent over. You tell me."

"The brochures were pretty impressive," Nat allowed.

Mr. Walsh said, "And this is the perfect place for

one of these things. You already have a well-established clientele, and this'll bring in new traffic. Believe me, Nat, that cash register is going to ring nonstop."

"Sounds good to me," Nat said.

Despite Mr. Walsh's enthusiasm, Nat still looked pensive. Brandon himself was not as certain of this as his dad. He remembered Mr. Walsh's previous obsessions—first the chord organ, then Brandon's basketball career, then competitive Christmas decorating. Mr. Walsh was generally a pretty stable guy, but every so often he went crazy—especially when a client was involved. It wasn't so much that he felt the necessity of using a client's product; Mr. Walsh just began to believe his own rhetoric. Hence the Peach Pit's new attraction.

Mr. Walsh said, "Brandon, make sure the whole crew is here tomorrow night when we crank up this baby." He smiled and swiveled his hips. "Because tomorrow night, we are going to rock and roll."

Brandon always got nervous when his father tried to act hip.

"You sure you can set this up alone?" Mr. Walsh asked.

"If the instructions are in English," Nat said, "we'll be fine."

Nat and Mr. Walsh shook hands, and then Mr. Walsh went home.

Putting the system together was not quite as easy as Nat had predicted, but in no more than a few hours it occupied a small stage area that had been ready for a week. Nat got himself and Brandon colas, and they drank while appraising their work.

"*Karaoke,*" Nat said as if trying the word for size. "*Karaoke.* Sounds like some kind of weird pudding, huh?"

Brandon was sitting at the other end of the room looking through the instructions. The whole thing still struck him as weird. Even if you could get somebody to sing in front of a bunch of strangers, what bunch of strangers would want to listen?

Brandon said, "It says here that literally translated from the Japanese, *karaoke* means 'empty orchestra.'"

"That makes sense," Nat said.

It made no sense to Brandon. He asked, "Are you sure this is a good idea?"

Nat shrugged and said tiredly, "You don't see the bills, kid. Between the money I spent on remodeling, and the money I lose because of this recession thing, I have to do something to bring in the people. I have the lunch traffic, but the night business ain't what it used to be."

"You said you had a good crowd tonight."

"Oh sure. Folks still drop by for a soda after a movie, but I want them to come here in the first place. You know, make a night of it."

"You think *karaoke* will do the trick?"

"Your dad swears by it."

Brandon knew that wasn't an answer, and he suspected that Nat knew it too. Besides, Brandon knew the kinds of things his dad swore by. He only hoped for Nat's sake that this time Dad's obsession was contagious.

Brenda felt that she'd never sweated so much in her life. Of course, that didn't prevent cardio-funk from being fun, but she couldn't deny it was also an awful lot of work—part dancing, part calisthenics, all business.

She knew she was getting soft, and Kelly looked as if she was, too. As always, no matter what she ate, Donna didn't gain an ounce of flab. It wasn't fair, but there it was.

Brenda had worked on Kelly for weeks before she agreed to accompany her to the class. For one thing, it was being held at the West Beverly gym. "Why go back to school when we don't have to?" Kelly asked. For another thing, Kelly's idea of exercise was signing her name to a credit card invoice.

Brenda believed that what had changed Kelly's mind at last were the neon tights they got to wear. Even in her present flab-ridden condition, Kelly looked great in tights. Rarely did Kelly pass up a chance to show off.

They had saved about a hundred bucks by buying the tights at the local dance shop at the mall instead of at Tracy Ross. That was one commission Diedre wouldn't get.

After all Brenda's work, here they were at last. True, the hardbodies around them were intimidating, and the slim black woman who was their instructor moved as if she'd been training since the cradle, but Brenda refused to go home just because she felt like a dork.

Kelly continued to complain, even as she gyrated and sweated. "I can't believe I'm jumping up and down with a room full of lonely people who can't get a date on a Friday night."

"Kelly, look around you. These are not lonely people. For instance, cast your Beverly Hills squinties on that guy over there."

The guy Brenda indicated with a nod of her head was not the hardest hunk in the class, and certainly not the best dancer. But he was handsome in a boyish and unassuming way, and he made his awkwardness work for him, as if he were doing it on purpose to get a laugh. And maybe he was. Brenda liked him immediately.

The guy saw Brenda and Kelly looking at him. Over the music he called, "Go ahead and laugh. They hired me for comic relief."

Brenda would have been worried that she'd embarrassed him by staring, but he was still smiling. He wasn't just cute. He was a big puppy of a guy. Brenda said, "No, no. You're doing great. Better than my friend here."

"Thanks a bunch," Kelly said.

"You must be a ringer," he said to Brenda.

This guy was great. Not only cute and floppy, but gallant. "Actually," Brenda said, "it's my first time."

"Now I'm really humiliated."

The instructor cried, "All right, boys and girls: Kicks! One two three four. Higher, boys and girls!"

"Great," said the guy. "She thinks we're the Rockettes."

"Tim, can we focus here?" the teacher called.

It turned out that Tim was the cute guy. As if he were attempting to pedal a bicycle up a hill, he called, "I'm focusing. I'm focusing."

"He's cute," Kelly said.

Adorable, Brenda thought. She said, "We're not here to meet guys, Kelly."

"Speak for yourself." She gave Tim a shot of her atomic smile.

Tim waved, but he continued to stare at Brenda. Brenda tried not to notice, but without success. After all, here was this great guy admiring her. She tried to do some focusing herself. She focused on Dylan.

The truth was, if Dylan hadn't started going to Friday night Alcoholics Anonymous meetings, she wouldn't even be here—flab or no flab. But she had to fill her Friday nights somehow or go crazy. Cardio-funk seemed like a good constructive thing to be doing while Dylan was doing *his* good constructive thing.

So, while Tim gazed at her, she thought about Dylan. Or tried to think about Dylan. She had a surprising amount of trouble focusing.

The instructor had them do some easier warm down exercises, and then a little deep breathing. By the time they were done, Brenda was ready for a warm bath and a soft bed.

Tim came over and said, "Hi. I'm Tim Matthews."

Brenda felt healthy, but too tired and sweaty to feel sexy. Tim didn't seem to notice. He had no trouble focusing on her. She introduced herself and Kelly. He was polite to Kelly, but Brenda was definitely the one he was interested in.

Brenda didn't know what to do. Guys had been interested in her before, of course, but never while she already had a boyfriend—someone who was theoretically the love of her life. The fact that she had used the word "theoretically," even in the privacy of her own brain, frightened her a little. Wasn't Dylan the love of her life? Still, shutting Tim down entirely would be rude. Brenda was never rude except when necessary.

"Let me guess," said Tim. He put his hand to his forehead like a stage mind reader. "Actress? Dancer? Star Search spokes-model?"

Brenda couldn't help laughing. "West Beverly High student."

"I'm at UCLA. Premed. But at the moment, the last thing I want to do is study organic chemistry. So would you guys maybe, possibly, like to get a bite to eat or something?"

Would she? Should she? She was abashed to find she was tempted. But it would never happen while her very own personal conscience, in the form of Kelly Taylor, was standing there. "Sorry," said Brenda. "Kelly's my ride. I have to go." She didn't move.

"I can drive you home."

Brenda glanced at Kelly. She was still glowering,

doing her best Jiminy Cricket impression. "Sorry," Brenda said.

"How about if I call you sometime?"

"I have a boyfriend."

"Dump him," Tim suggested joyfully.

"Brenda, I have to be home," Kelly said.

Thanks Jiminy.

Tim said, "See you Sunday, then."

Sunday? Brenda knew there was another cardio-funk class on Sunday night, but she had never even considered taking it. Could she do this twice a week and live? Besides, why would she want to tie herself up on a night when Dylan was free?

Brenda was surprised to hear herself say, "Sure. See you then."

As she hustled Brenda toward the locker room, Kelly said, "I thought we were only coming once a week, when Dylan's at AA."

"I was thinking I need a little more exercise."

"An exercise named Tim?"

"Kelly," Brenda cried. She was horrified that what Kelly said might be true. What about Dylan? "I was just being polite."

"I hope Tim was able to make the subtle distinction between polite and coming on strong."

"I told him I have a boyfriend. And I didn't give him my number."

"What if I hadn't been standing there?"

"Listen, Jiminy Cricket, I came here to exercise. I exercised. What's it to you or anybody else if I made a new friend at the same time?"

Kelly looked at her with wild speculation.

"Let's get out of these sweaty tights," Brenda said. She hoped the subject was changed permanently. This whole discussion made her nervous.

Dylan always enjoyed the drive from Beverly Hills to Malibu. Driving along the coast was boss, of course, not only because he was near the ocean, but because the air down here was cleaner than it was even a few miles inland. It smelled of salt water and seaweed—two smells that always cranked Dylan, especially at night.

He didn't think that going to an Alcoholics Anonymous meeting made him better than other people, but he felt good about getting his life in order.

His mom was a nutbar who lived in Hawaii. His father was in jail for a white-collar crime so convoluted that only three people at the Securities and Exchange Commission understood it. He didn't exactly have the perfect family life.

He could sit around crying about it, he could go over the edge himself, or he could actually take his own life in his two hands and make something of himself. He could become a *mensch*, as Andrea Zuckerman had suggested. *Mensch* was Yiddish for man, but it meant a lot more than that. It also meant somebody who was responsible for his own life and who did a good job with it. A woman could be a *mensch*, and Dylan knew many of them who were.

The Malibu AA meeting was held in a public recreation room on the beach. It was painted government green, and it was not very fancy. But nobody was there for the atmosphere. They were there for the meeting.

The room was almost full by the time Dylan walked in. Guys in suits sat shoulder to shoulder with housewives and with surf bums who looked as if they didn't have two nickels to rub together. He sat down next to Ben, his sponsor. Ben was a great guy. He'd been through some very tough times, but he'd been dry for years, and now had his own small business.

The first speaker was a blond girl. She was pretty, if a little fragile, and Dylan was astonished that he knew her. Her name was Sarah, but back in her drinking days she was known to her surf acquaintances—none of them were really her friends—as Betty. Once, she'd tried to swim while loaded, and had almost drowned. Brandon Walsh had pulled her out of the ocean, and Brenda had called an ambulance. They'd saved Sarah's life. Dylan had never seen her at an AA meeting.

Sarah began with the traditional greeting. "My name is Sarah, and I'm an alcoholic."

Everybody in the audience said, "Hello, Sarah."

"I've been sober fifty days now. Unfortunately, they've been spread out over the last four years."

That got a laugh. Nobody thought Sarah's problems were funny; the laughter was born of recognition. Many of the group had had similar problems, and worse. Humor helped them deal with their lives.

Sarah said, "I hung out with a pretty tough crowd when I was twelve. I was never very comfortable with them or with myself, and drinking helped me fit in. I was drunk at school a lot and one time I even tossed my cookies right in the principal's office."

A lot of people nodded at that, and some laughed. Dylan remembered the few times he'd been drunk at school. Nothing bothered him while he was drunk, but afterward, during the hangover, he squirmed with embarrassment at what he had done and said. He squirmed now with the memory.

"I thought I hit bottom last year when I almost drowned while surfing with a snootful. If it wasn't for a couple of high school kids, I'd be dead now. But I kept drinking. My parents didn't know what to do with me, so they threw me out. 'Tough love,' and all that garbage. I met this guy and he moved in with me. All we did was drink. And then he beat me up pretty bad, and that scared me bad enough to send me back here. I've been sober for about a week now. I guess it's a start."

Dylan applauded along with everybody else. There wasn't one person in the room who didn't know how difficult it was to stay sober that first week, that first day, that first hour. Each person had to work their program alone, but that didn't mean they couldn't applaud Sarah for doing a good job.

There were three other speakers that evening: a

network executive named Jim; a convenience store clerk named Anton; and Michelle, a mother of two small children. Their stories were harrowing, but the fact that they were here, and had been coming here for some time, caused Dylan to believe that their lives had turned around.

During the last item of the formal meeting, Dylan was presented with a chip signifying ninety days of sobriety. Everyone had coffee, and Dylan had a chance to speak with Sarah. She had a lot of potential as a woman, Dylan thought. And while he didn't have any romantic intentions toward her, he did enjoy her company. Nothing wrong with that.

"How are you doing?" Dylan asked.

"Better than last time you saw me, when that guy and his sister saved my life."

"Brandon and Brenda, yeah. They do good work."

Sarah seemed embarrassed that anybody would think of saving her life as good work. This woman needed some new tread on her ego. Maybe he could help.

"So, you still surfing?" Sarah asked.

"All the time."

"I was thinking of getting back into it. Maybe the salt water'll wash some of this muck out of my brain."

Here was Dylan's chance. He said, "Waves are up. I'm going out tomorrow morning if you want to meet me."

Dylan's suggestion seemed to astonish her. "Yeah?" she said. "Maybe I will."

"Be the best thing for you." It was certainly the best thing for him. Ice hockey was all very well, but there was nothing like the slamma jamma of surfing.

When the meeting broke up, Dylan asked if Sarah needed a ride home. She said she didn't and then hiked off into the darkness. He wondered how far away she lived, and if she had a vehicle parked out there somewhere.

Bad thinking. He couldn't kidnap her, not even to do her a favor. He'd had plenty of experience with people who thought they knew better than he did. They gave him a pain. If the girl wanted to walk home, or take the bus, or whatever, that was up to her.

He suddenly had a powerful urge to see Brenda—not only so he could show her his ninety-day chip, but because he needed to know that she was still there for him. Despite appearances, he was as insecure as anybody else, maybe more so.

He knew that everybody at school thought of him as cool and almost indestructible, but the truth was, he was just distant. His parents had taught him by example that getting too close was a mistake. He hoped that his relationship with Brenda would teach him that there was no such thing as getting too close. He liked Brenda as much as any girl he'd ever known, but getting close still made him uncomfortable. Well, this stuff didn't happen over night.

He revved his Porsche and drove out onto Pacific Coast Highway. He enjoyed the wind, full of the sea, blowing in his face. When he had to turn inland, the sea breeze went away, and he was just driving. He enjoyed just driving, but it wasn't the same.

He drove up through the wide quiet streets of Beverly Hills and stopped in front of the Walsh home. He sat in the car for a while because the hour was late and he wasn't certain that a visit would be appreciated. A light was on in the living room. Maybe somebody was watching the news or dozing over a book.

He gently knocked on the door. Somebody looked out at him through the fisheye, and then opened the door. It was Brenda. She looked very cute in her red Lantz nightgown. She assured him that it was not too late to visit.

"How was your class?" Dylan asked.

"Okay," Brenda said. She shrugged. "You know. A lot of sweaty lonely people who didn't have a date on a Friday night. How was your meeting?"

He pulled the chip from his jacket pocket, held it up and turned it in the light coming from the foyer. It looked like a poker chip, a piece of cheap plastic, but it was symbolic of a life under control. He said, "Ninety days of sobriety, Bren." It was one of the proudest things he'd ever said.

Brenda seemed to understand his feelings. She touched the chip as if it were gold, and said, "I had no idea. I'm so proud of you, Dylan."

He knew that not drinking was a big deal, but Brenda's fuss embarrassed him. He said, "Maybe you should come with me to a meeting."

"I'd love to."

Dylan knew she wouldn't love to. Until they actually visited an AA meeting, most people reacted to an invitation as if they'd been invited to a hospital for AIDS patients. But if he was going to share his life with this woman, it was important she share a few AA meetings with him. She had to know what they were like.

"Okay," said Dylan. "What about Sunday?"

"This Sunday?" Brenda asked with some surprise.

"It's okay if you can't," Dylan said.

"No, no. I'll cancel this other thing. I'd love to come."

"Thanks. It would mean a lot to me."

Neither of them spoke. Dylan felt that something had gone unsaid, but he didn't know what it was. He'd spoken with Sarah at the meeting, but what of it? He spoke to women all the time.

"Do you want to come in for a while?" Brenda asked.

The moment of nervousness was broken. Dylan was pleased to have a subject again. He said, "No thanks. I have to get up early tomorrow if I'm going to catch the good surf. I have to get it while they got it." He wondered if Sarah would show up. Surfing would be good for her.

Evidently, Brenda was not yet comfortable with the conversation. She still had something on her mind. She looked at the step when she said, "Dylan, have you noticed that our lives seem to be going in two different directions?"

To Dylan, this sounded like a girl who was thinking about breaking up. Had something happened at that cardio-funk class? The world was full of hunks without shirts. He tried to stay calm when he said, "Not any more than usual. Why?"

"I don't know. We seem to have less and less in common."

"What are we, joined at the hip? You worry too much."

"Maybe." She smiled without certainty.

Dylan knew that people drifted apart, but he and Brenda had more important things in common than whether she surfed or not.

They kissed good night. Then Brenda congratulated him again on his ninety days, and closed the door. He stood for a moment wondering what their conversation had been all about. Not about its words, that was for sure. They'd skated over the surface of something ugly.

7

Busting out

—

DYLAN GOT TO THE BEACH THE NEXT MORNING just after the sun came up. He sat on a dune admiring the shape of the waves while the cold wind blew around him. There was nothing like the beach in the morning. It was easy to believe the world belonged to him alone.

"Hi, stranger," somebody called.

Sarah walked toward him, carrying her board and filling out her wet suit very nicely. Dylan figured that the chances of her showing up were fifty-fifty, and he was glad to see her. The surfing would be therapeutic for both of them.

They surfed for a while and the water was good. But the cold seeped into Dylan through his wet suit, and when the sun was about two fists high, he suggested they stop for coffee. Sarah eagerly agreed.

They sat on the beach enjoying each other's company. Sarah told Dylan the same old story, how she thought she had to get drunk to have a good time, how drinking on the beach seemed so natural.

"That's what civilians don't understand," Dylan said. He stared out at the water, and saw that the shape of the waves was blowing away. Unless they wanted to be satisfied with waves that were only okay instead of great, surfing was over for the day.

Dylan was pleased to hear that Sarah had a job at a beauty parlor, and was studying to get her haircutting license.

"You want to cut my hair?" Dylan asked and grinned.

She grabbed for his hair, and they ended up tussling in the sand. They stopped just short of kissing. Dylan had to think of Brenda. It would be unfair to lead this girl on. It would be unfair to him, too. Brenda had a right to expect a certain amount of loyalty from him, just as he had a right to expect it from her.

They packed their stuff and walked up the beach to their cars. Dylan had long since stopped apologizing for driving a Porsche—for him, it was just transportation—but Sarah seemed embarrassed by the fact that she drove a battered old Japanese box.

He walked her to her car, and stood so that she had her back to the Porsche. She smiled at him and said, "So, like, I was wondering, do you want to go to a movie or something tonight?"

Dylan had been afraid for hours she might ask just such a question. He had no illusions about being a great catch, but he could guess how fragile Sarah was right now. She would fall into the arms of any guy who paid attention to her. He liked her but he didn't want to be that guy.

As gently as possible, Dylan said, "I'm sorry, Sarah. I already have plans."

She nodded as she chewed on her lip. Dylan didn't want to reinforce her feeling that she wasn't worth going out with, but he'd promised Brenda he would go to that damned *karaoke* thing that evening. Besides, Sarah becoming codependent on Dylan would be a bad thing for both of them.

"No sweat," said Sarah. "I'll find something to do. I just don't feel like being by myself these days."

"I understand. You could always go to a meeting."

"Two nights in a row?"

"Whatever works."

Sarah made no comment and Dylan didn't want to pressure her. That wasn't what AA was all about. While he watched her drive away, he wondered if even surfing with Sarah was a good idea.

Outside a sporting event, Brandon had rarely seen his dad so excited. Brandon was a little excited himself. He and Nat had tried *karaoke* the night before after setting it up, and Brandon had to admit that pretending you were Mick Jagger could be lots of fun.

At dinner, Mr. Walsh could speak about nothing but *karaoke*. Brandon and Brenda reported that all their friends would be at the Peach Pit that evening.

"Great," Mr. Walsh said. "My clients tell me the bigger the crowd, the better. Get people to try *karaoke* once, and they're hooked." He held a fork as if it were a microphone and began to sing "Do Wah Diddy."

Mrs. Walsh looked at her husband with concern. She said, "You're not actually going to get up there and sing, are you?"

"Of course I am. If I don't, how can I expect anybody else to give it a try?"

"Don't worry, Mom," Brenda said. "You'll only be humiliated in front of a hundred of your closest friends."

The phone rang and Mrs. Walsh went to answer it. "Hello? Yes, she's right here. Who's calling, please?" She put her hand over the receiver and said, "Brenda, it's Tim Matthews."

Brenda froze. The expression of horror on her face was pretty entertaining, and Brandon settled down to see what would happen next.

"Tell him I'm not here."

"I already told him you were right here. Come on, he sounds like a very nice boy."

Brenda took the phone, and the rest of them

tried to pretend they were interested in their food, but they were listening, and Brenda surely knew they were listening.

On the other end of the phone was a guy obviously asking for a date. It was also obvious from Brenda's flirtatious attitude that despite the fact she turned him down, she liked him. She hung up and went back to her dinner as if nothing had happened. She looked around the table and saw that everybody was staring at her.

"What?" asked Brenda.

"Nothing," said Mr. Walsh, and he was off and running on *karaoke* again.

Brandon could not help being curious who Tim Matthews was, but he knew better than to ask Brenda a direct question. Few things would make Brenda more secretive than a direct question. Besides, Brandon knew that if Brenda was interested in him, Tim would show up at the house eventually. Brandon hoped only that Tim would not be a problem for Dylan.

When dinner was over, they all piled into Dad's car. Dad turned on his radio and one of the oldies stations came up. He rocked with anything the station played. He was so into the music that he almost had an accident. Mrs. Walsh had to remind him twice to keep his mind on his driving.

Brenda had never seen her father like this. He seemed to have lost his mind entirely. Evidently, Nat had lost his mind too. Generally, the Peach Pit was an unpretentious little diner; the food was good and the floor show consisted of a jukebox full of Nat's favorite songs.

But tonight, Brenda was surprised to see searchlights in the street out in front, and in the window, surrounded by flashing lights, was a sign that announced *KARAOKE TONIGHT*! The sidewalk was crowded with people looking in the windows and on their way in the door. Brenda was a little saddened by all the commotion. She was pleased that Nat was doing so well, of course, but it was pretty obvious that the Pit was no longer the secret hangout of just her and her friends.

Mr. Walsh had trouble finding a place to park, but at last he found a spot on the street a few blocks away. As Mr. Walsh led the parade back to the Peach Pit, Brenda whispered to Brandon, "I've never seen Dad so stoked."

"Yeah. Dad's really ready to rock and roll."

"You don't think this is weird?"

"Sure it's weird. I think that's part of the appeal. Remember, Dad's a guy who wears a suit and tie all day."

Brandon was probably right. This was Dad's big chance to bust out in a socially acceptable way. She hoped it would be socially acceptable. Who knew what he would do when he got up to sing in front of a group of strangers?

The Peach Pit was so packed that the serving people on duty had trouble getting through the crush with their orders. A hand reached out and grabbed Brenda. She was startled and momentarily frightened, and then she saw the person who'd grabbed her was Dylan. He was standing next to the door with a bemused smile on his face. Brandon looked back at him and gave him the thumbs-up. Dylan nodded.

"Quite a gala," Dylan said.

"Are you going to sing?" Brenda asked.

"Not unless you hold a gun to my head."

Nat, for the occasion dressed in a white tuxedo, leaped onto the stage with a microphone in his hand. He was beaming. Brenda knew that Nat had done a little acting early in his life—some extra work in westerns and gangster pictures—and his theatrical inclination showed now. Behind him was a banner that said CAN YOU KARAOKE?

Nat thanked everybody for coming, and then he invited her father to the stage to kick off *karaoke* at the Peach Pit. "After all," Nat said, "it was his idea."

Mr. Walsh joined Nat on stage, cried, "Hit it, maestro," and began to sing "Do Wah Diddy."

Mrs. Walsh buried her head in her hands, but everybody else seemed to appreciate Mr. Walsh's efforts. They clapped and bopped in time.

"Do Wah Diddy" was the hit of the evening, and soon other people got up to sing it solo, or in duets, trios, and even quartets. Brenda couldn't stand just watching any more. She grabbed Dylan firmly by the hand and pulled him across the room to the stage. He fought her only briefly. At first he was pretty stiff on stage, but he loosened up, and began to groove with Brenda, Kelly, and Donna.

When Mr. Walsh got up again and began to sing "That Old Black Magic," Brenda knew the evening was winding down and it was time to leave. She approached her mom, who was watching Mr. Walsh with a fearful skepticism, and spoke directly into her ear to be heard over the music. "Dylan's going to drive me home."

Without turning away from the stage, Mrs. Walsh nodded.

On the way to Dylan's house, they agreed that Mr. Walsh actually sang pretty well for somebody who was not only an old guy but a dad. Dylan shook his head and said, "I've never seen so many sober people acting so stupid in my life."

"You sang, too," Brenda said.

"Sure. Because somebody—who shall remain nameless—dragged me up onto the stage. It was either sing or pretend I was a potted palm."

Dylan was not really upset that he'd been forced to sing. If somebody had shoved bamboo shoots under his fingernails, he eventually would have admitted that he'd had a good time. But he was glad the public part of the evening was over and he could have Brenda to himself. Life was good. He wondered how Sarah was doing this evening, and he frowned.

"What?" Brenda asked.

"Nothing," Dylan said.

At home, Dylan had barely closed the door when Brenda wrapped herself around him and began a long, slowly grinding kiss. She felt good against him, and he responded without thought—all hormones and instincts.

Suddenly, Brenda pulled away and said, "Your answering machine is blinking."

Dylan was a little disoriented, as if someone had awakened him by turning over the bed. As he reached for her, he said, "Can't be important. I just saw everybody I know on this planet."

"You never know," Brenda said. She touched the playback button.

The first message was from Brandon, reminding Dylan that this was *karaoke* night.

"You see?" Dylan said. "Old news."

But the second message got Dylan's full attention. He listened with a mixture of embarrassment and concern, aware that Brenda was standing next to him, a neutral expression on her face. The message was from Sarah. "I'm not doing so good tonight, Dylan. In fact, I need a drink pretty bad. Please call me. Please." The fact was, she sounded shaky and weak.

Dylan didn't understand why he felt so damn guilty. People in AA got this kind of phone call all the time. In fact, to give and get support was one of the reasons AA existed. If that was the case, why did he feel so guilty? "I should take care of this," he said.

Brenda said that she understood, and maybe she did, but Dylan was having trouble sorting out his own motives. He had to help Sarah, no question about that. But he couldn't decide whether something else was going on, too.

He called Sarah and found out that Doug was there. Doug was the guy who got her drinking again, and who'd beaten her up: obviously one hundred percent slime. Sarah sounded frightened, and she hung up after once again pleading with Dylan to come over.

Dylan drove Brenda home, and then drove over the hill to the valley as quickly as he could without breaking any speed laws.

Sarah lived in the back apartment of a tacky building in Van Nuys. Dylan walked along the balcony and stopped in front of her door. All was quiet. He took a deep breath and looked down into the patio where a swimming pool with masses of dead leaves on the bottom shimmered in the yellow porch lights. Dylan knew that he had a reputation for acting like the Lone Ranger—saving the weak and innocent from tough situations, and then leaving. Despite his reputation, Dylan hated confrontations. That's one of the reasons he acted so tough, to deflect confrontations with people who might otherwise mess with him.

But Dylan could see no way to avoid this one. If Sarah was right about Doug, he was unlikely to leave without some encouragement. Dylan sighed and knocked on Sarah's door.

Someone peeked out, and then Sarah opened the door wide enough for Dylan to enter. She was nervous and looked thinner than she had that morning at the beach. On the sagging couch was Doug, a big slug of a man showing hair and pale skin between the top of his dirty jeans and the bottom of his Dead Kennedys t-shirt. He held a half full bottle of beer in one hand. Empty bottles were all around him, brown and shiny as cockroaches. The guy seemed unaware of anything, including the fact that Dylan was there. Dylan was disgusted.

Sarah said, "He won't leave, Dylan. And if he stays I'm afraid I'll take that bottle out of his hand and drink the rest of it myself."

Dylan didn't want to touch the guy, but he went over and grabbed Doug by the arm and pulled him to his feet. His skin was cool and damp. Doug was surprised and then angry. He swayed as if in a high wind. "Who the hell are you?"

"I'm a friend of Sarah's," Dylan said. "Why don't you just take your bottle and go somewhere else?"

Dylan's request seemed to puzzle Doug for a moment. Then he said, "The sobriety patrol, huh? Didn't know you guys made house calls." He leered. "Or is that just for blondes?"

Doug's comment stung Dylan. He was there primarily as a fellow AA member, but he could not deny the fact that he liked Sarah as a person. She was very cute and she needed help—two characteristics that always attracted his attention. He didn't bring home stray animals, but the impulse was there. The Lone Ranger probably collected stray animals, too.

Angrily, Dylan gripped Doug by a belt loop and the back of his shirt and hustled him toward the door. Doug shook him off and turned, breathing hard, looking to Dylan like an enraged bear.

Dylan appraised him while he waited for the attack. Doug was unsteady on his feet, and certainly not trained in hand-to-hand combat, but he was enormous, and probably so drunk as to be entirely without fear. Dylan guessed he could take Doug if necessary, but it would be a lot of work.

But Doug only said, "You don't have to shove me. I'm going." He looked at Sarah with contempt and said, "You can have her. She ain't worth fighting over." He went out and slammed the door.

Sarah collapsed into Dylan's arms and he was a little scared because she felt as if she belonged there. She began to cry. He smoothed her hair gently and told her that everything was going to be all right, though he was far from certain that it would be. When Doug sobered up, or at least got less drunk, he would probably be back. And he was likely to bring friends.

They stood there like that for a long time, and it slowly occurred to Dylan that he would have to stay the night.

8

The
program

BRENDA GOT UP QUICKLY THE NEXT MORNING because she'd invited Kelly over to jog. She wasn't sure where her new interest in physical fitness came from, but she doubted if it had anything to do with Tim Matthews. After all, she'd signed up for cardio-funk before she met him.

No, she just wanted to get into shape. Flab was so unattractive.

She pulled on her shorts and her tank top. While she tied her running shoes, she wondered again where Dylan had been when she'd called late the night before. She looked at the clock. It was a

Shaking on it. Ian Ziering as Steve Sanders, Luke Perry as Dylan McKay, and Jason Priestley as Brandon Walsh.

Brenda Walsh as played by Shannen Doherty.

Jennie Garth as Kelly Taylor.

Man-about-town Steve Sanders, played by Ian Ziering.

Donna Martin as played by Tori Spelling.

Gabrielle Carteris flashes Andrea Zuckerman's brilliant smile.

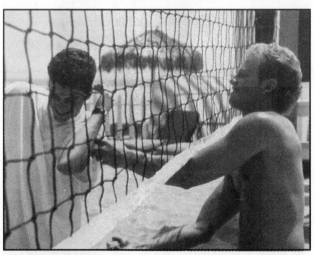

David Silver (Brian Austin Green) tries to dodge Steve Sanders (Ian Ziering).

Brandon Walsh as played by Jason Priestley.

Love will keep them together. Luke Perry and Shannen Doherty as Dylan McKay and Brenda Walsh.

Luke Perry as Dylan McKay.

The hip, hot cast of *"90210"*. *From left:* Ian Ziering, Tori Spelling, Luke Perry, Gabrielle Carteris, Shannen Doherty, Jason Priestley, Jennie Garth, and Brian Austin Green.

little early for Dylan to be up, but she really had to talk to him. She called his house and got the machine again. She didn't even leave a message. Honest concern was one thing, but there was no point giving Dylan the impression she was frantic.

Kelly showed up in a red outfit that had white racing stripes. They went out and jogged. Kelly seemed very intent on what she was doing, which was all right with Brenda. She was busy thinking about Dylan and Sarah.

Brenda understood that outreach was a feature of Dylan's AA program, but the hard part was that Brenda knew Sarah. She'd even saved Sarah's life. Maybe that had been a mistake. Brenda was immediately upset that she could even think such things. The point was that knowing Sarah made it more difficult for Brenda to accept the fact that Dylan's interest in her was entirely AA related. After all, Sarah was cute, and Dylan was only human.

She couldn't ask him where he'd been, of course. She wanted to see how long Dylan took before he mentioned it, if ever. If she believed Kelly, Brenda had stuff she ought to mention to Dylan, but her case was entirely different. For one thing, Brenda did not receive wild phone calls from Tim asking for help. Nothing was going on between them. Tim was just some guy she'd met in exercise class.

When she and Kelly got back to the house, the entire family was in the kitchen eating breakfast. Her father was holding a banana to her mother's mouth as if it were a microphone, trying to get her to sing "Do Wah Diddy" along with him. She pushed the banana away.

Brenda could see her mom had had about enough of *karaoke,* but Dad didn't notice.

Dylan had not called while Brenda was out, but Tim had. Kelly was surprised that Tim had her number, and her tone led Brenda to believe that she did not approve. Kelly had nothing to worry about, of course. Tim was just some guy from exercise class.

Brenda's big worry was Brandon. Brandon and Dylan hung out together a lot, and Brandon would have plenty of opportunity to tell Dylan about this phone call. Brandon promised that he wouldn't. He might not do it on purpose, but sometimes things slipped out. If Tim was just a guy from exercise class, why did it matter?

Dylan awoke the next morning to the tiny mouse sounds of somebody moving stuff around nearby. He opened one eye and saw Sarah pushing old fast-food wrappers and beer bottles off the coffee table. Dylan remembered that at Sarah's insistence, he'd stayed over at her apartment. "In case Doug comes back." At his own insistence, he slept on the couch, not in her bed.

As he sat up and rubbed his eyes, Sarah explained that she'd made him breakfast in bed, "or at least in couch," to thank him for not leaving her alone.

Dylan blinked at what she'd set down on the coffee table: scrambled eggs and a couple of wedges of dark toast. No coffee, but the cola probably had some caffeine in it. Pretty basic, but it would do. Something to prime the old pump.

Sarah sat down next to Dylan and said, "I have something else for you, too."

He turned his head to ask what it was, and ran into a kiss. It was a good kiss, and Dylan enjoyed it. But the longer it went on, the more concerned he became about where this relationship was going.

Dylan gently pushed her away and said, "This isn't a good idea."

"Why not? You surf and you're sober. I think it's a great idea."

Dylan looked at her steadily. Time for the shock treatment. He said, "I have a girlfriend, Sarah."

"Oh."

"I know I should have told you sooner."

"Yeah."

"I'm sorry."

She laid her head on Dylan's shoulder. "I can't go through this alone, Dylan. I'm scared. I'm scared I'll just slide away."

"You won't. You're not alone. Go to the meeting tonight. I'll be there, too. I promise."

Dylan was also scared. Before meeting Sarah he was convinced that Brenda was his one true love; but now he wasn't so sure. Here was this poor frightened creature who needed him. The question of whether he needed her was still open. But asking the question at all started him thinking about things he previously had taken for granted.

Though it was Sunday and he really wasn't busy, he left Sarah's apartment as soon as he could. He didn't know whether being alone was the best thing for her right now, but he did know that they should not hang around together. Let her call some other AA member. He wanted to help, but he didn't want either of them to get burned.

Dylan went to the beach and sat watching the waves for a while, then drove up to Will Rogers Park where he hiked along the trails. He even took the tour of the house and left a few bucks in the kitty. He stood on the berm of a big square field and watched the polo players knock the ball around.

Later, he drove back down to the Peach Pit for a burger. The *karaoke* was unemployed at the moment, and the equipment looked like an abandoned city.

"Want to sing a song?" Nat asked.

"No thanks. Brandon doesn't dance, and I don't sing."

"Besides," said Nat mournfully, "if you're going to sing in an empty room, you might as well do it at home."

"I thought the *karaoke* machine was supposed to bring in customers."

"Oh, it brings them in at night. But some Sunday afternoons are so dead, not even the Baron Frankenstein could make them live."

Dylan nodded as he ate his burger. He mused

over Brenda and Sarah again, found that he still didn't have an answer, and decided to give it a rest.

He dawdled over his food, drove around for a while, and then went to pick up Brenda for the AA meeting. She was dressed as if for church, which was a little on the fancy side for the gig, but some people did dress up for meetings, so Dylan let it go.

The drive to Malibu was exhilarating as usual, and the meeting was about normal for a Sunday night, full of alcoholics congratulating themselves for making it through another weekend without a drink.

Brenda watched and listened with eager interest, but Dylan didn't really know what she made of the meeting till it was over and he had a chance to ask.

"Things get really personal," she said. "I mean, people talk about everything. I thought they would just talk about drinking."

"Sharing secrets makes life less painful, Bren. And if you're in a little less pain, maybe you won't drink."

While she nodded, Ben, Dylan's sponsor, walked over to meet Brenda. They made small talk for a few minutes, and then Dylan worked up his nerve to ask, "Ben, have you seen Sarah?" He felt funny to be talking about Sarah in front of Brenda.

Ben said that he hadn't.

Dylan said, "She said she'd be at the meeting tonight, but she never showed. I'm kind of worried about her."

"Listen," said Ben, "you work *your* program, and let Sarah work *hers*."

Dylan looked at the floor while he considered what Ben said. "I guess you're right," he said.

Brenda had heard a lot about Sarah lately, and though she did not wish the girl any harm, Brenda also was a little bored by all the talk. Ben's advice made her happy, and confirmed the little she knew about the Alcoholics Anonymous program. Maybe now Dylan would pay more attention to her.

They were supposed to meet Kelly at the Peach Pit after the meeting. She would be there after cardio-funk, undoubtedly replenishing her bodily fluids with a milk shake. "Food without guilt," is what she called anything she ate after the exercise class.

From outside the Peach Pit, Brenda was afraid she recognized the voice of the person working out on the *karaoke* machine. The door opened, she could see across to the stage, and she knew she was right. It was her father, mangling "Be Bop A Lula." Evidently, he favored songs that had nonsense syllables for titles. Her mother, Brandon, and Nat were at the counter, watching Mr. Walsh with a mixture of horror and amazement.

And then Brenda saw something even more frightening than her father singing in public. There was Tim Matthews sitting next to Kelly. The shock almost made her turn around and guide Dylan back into the parking lot, but after all, Tim was nothing special. He was just some guy in her cardio-funk class.

Tim saw them enter and came over. His smile was large and sincere, but Dylan had no expression at all on his face. "Who's he?" Dylan asked.

"Just some guy I met at my exercise class."

"You never mentioned him."

Brenda almost screamed at Dylan that there was nothing to mention. And how about that alcoholic bimbo you picked up? she wanted to shout. But she didn't. She concentrated on stretching the limits of her social skills instead. Donna said that she sometimes dreamed of two hunks fighting over her. This had never been a dream of Brenda's, and yet in the next few minutes, it was likely to happen. She felt very tense.

Tim said, "Hi. Kelly told me you might be here." He concentrated on Brenda. Dylan might as well have been invisible.

It was now obvious to her that Kelly had engineered this meeting in the hopes of forcing Brenda to make some kind of choice between Dylan and Tim. Of course, only one choice was possible. Of course. Dylan was not the type who fought without reason, and Brenda didn't think that Tim was the type either, but the way they were sizing each other up, anything could happen. This was all flattering, of course. Why wasn't she enjoying it more?

Brenda said, "Dylan McKay, this is Tim Matthews."

Each shook hands as if suspecting the other carried the plague.

Dylan said, "So, you guys met in some aerobics class?"

"Cardio-funk, actually," Tim said. "Really raises the old heart rate." He held out his wrist to Brenda and like a vaudeville comedian said, "Take my pulse—please!"

Brenda laughed and then explained to Dylan, "Tim is premed." Tim was so funny and cute. Dylan went in more for mystery than for puppy-dog charm, but at the moment he seemed preoccupied with something other than possible competition for Brenda.

Dylan said, "Yeah. Premed. Right. Listen, would you excuse me? I have to call somebody."

Brenda realized that Dylan was not making much of a showing against Tim. Against her will, she wondered if her continuing fidelity was worth the trouble.

"Now?" she asked.

"I want to try Sarah one more time. Maybe she came in."

That bitch. Calmly, Brenda said, "Okay. Whatever." She wanted to smile at Tim, but she controlled herself.

Dylan promised to be right back, and headed for the public phones at the back of the diner.

Brenda introduced Tim to her mom. Evidently, Kelly had already introduced him to Brandon. She would have to thank Kelly for bringing Tim here. Something with poison in it seemed about right.

"And that's my father," Brenda said. She gestured to the stage where Mr. Walsh was still in the throes of "Be Bop A Lula."

"Wow," said Tim. "The whole family's here, huh?" He sounded impressed.

"Sure," said Brenda. "The family that *karaokes* together stays together. Or something like that." Tim smiled and she went on, "*You* try to find a rhyme for *karaoke*."

"Not me," Tim said. "I'm more into macrame."

Mrs. Walsh was watching her husband again. She shook her head and said, "He's been at it all night."

"Time for a break, huh?" Tim said.

Mrs. Walsh nodded and said, "For us, for him, for the room."

"I know what to do. Come on, Brenda, let's show them how it's done."

As Tim pulled Brenda toward the *karaoke* stage, she wondered where Dylan was, and why he was allowing this strange guy to steal her away. And then her analytical thoughts dissolved in the fun of singing "Wild Thing" with Tim. He could actually sing pretty well, and when he did his Mick Jagger impression––all lips and tongue—she couldn't help laughing.

Brenda was tossing her hair back like Cher when she noticed Dylan motioning to her. She couldn't tell if he was angry or just concerned, but she was actually hoping for anger. At least that would mean she still meant something to him.

She was still laughing when she got to him and said, "He dragged me up there. Sorry."

"Forget it," Dylan said. He barely even looked at

her. His mind was somewhere else. "I couldn't get hold of Sarah."

"Oh?" It was a very cold *oh* and Brenda meant it to be.

"She was really on the edge last night, and I'm worried. I have to go over there and see what's happening."

"What about what Ben said? You know, letting her work her own program?"

"Ben didn't mean I should allow some ugly slug to use her for a punching bag. I can't let her down now, Bren. She's counting on me."

This all sounded damned suspicious to Brenda. Dylan seemed sincere, and maybe he was. But even so, Brenda believed he was kidding himself. He really liked this girl, and he was using AA as an excuse to see her. Brenda feared that if Dylan wanted to leave, there was no way she could stop him. She was sure that an argument wouldn't help. Not now. Not here. For the moment, she would be understanding. Having Tim around made that a lot easier. Maybe Tim made it too easy.

She said, "Okay. You have to do what you have to do."

Dylan put his hands on her shoulders. Brenda noticed that it was not quite a hug—more the kind of thing Brandon might do. Dylan said, "You know I'd rather stay here with you."

"Whatever."

Brenda was pleased to see worry flash across Dylan's face. "Bren—" he said.

"Just go. It's all right. I understand."

Dylan nodded, glanced at Tim, who had been standing to one side pretending to be interested in a menu, and left quickly. Brenda wondered for about the millionth time why even the most desirable guys could be such jerks.

Tim came up next to her and said, "If that was your ride, I'm available."

Her parents were here, and so was Brandon. Plus the fact that each of her friends had a car. She was not exactly short of rides. But she needed an emotional lift right now as well as a lift home, and she felt that only Tim would be able to give her that.

She smiled at him and said, "Sure. Let's go."

Tim drove an old Volkswagen bug, and they had to shout to be heard over the lawn-mower engine that powered it. They laughed about her dad's enthusiasm for *karaoke*, and how he'd sung himself hoarse. Tim was a wonderful guy. He was a good listener and had an outrageous sense of humor.

And what was Dylan? He was Dylan. At one time, that had been enough for Brenda. No further explanations had been necessary. Now Brenda wasn't so sure.

When they got to her house, the only lights showing were in her parents' bedroom. The backs of their hands brushed against each other as Tim walked Brenda to the front door. They talked for a while about the fun they'd had that evening. Dylan's name did not come up. Brenda was aware that they were getting closer together, and at last Tim kissed her.

She let the kiss happen, first, to see if Tim was a good kisser, and second, to teach Dylan a lesson; Tim was a very good kisser, and she enjoyed it. Then suddenly she pulled away, a little breathless.

"I shouldn't be doing this," Brenda said.

"I know," Tim said, "you have a boyfriend. If you want, I'll go away and never talk to you again. But you have to tell me to do it."

Brenda found that she couldn't do it, but when she said, "I can't," she meant something else. "I can't do this. I don't mean to lead you on."

"You're not."

Brenda didn't know if it was possible to love two guys at once. Maybe Kelly knew, or her mom. Of course, she could never ask either of them. It would be too incriminating. "Good night, then," she said, and turned toward the door with her key.

"Think about going out with me. That's all I ask."

"All right."

"Promise?"

She would anyway. She might as well promise. She did.

Tim said, "I like you, Brenda Walsh," and then walked quickly across the lawn. He gave her a jaunty wave, got into the car and drove away.

Brenda stood on the porch for a long time wondering what she was going to do.

*   *   *

Dylan didn't know what to expect at Sarah's house. She might not be home. She might have a headache and simply not be answering the phone. She might be lying dead in a puddle of blood. Anything was possible. There was no point thinking about it. The drive to the valley seemed to take a long time.

He found a place to park and ran up the stairs to her apartment. Lights were on, but no sound came from inside, not even music. He knocked politely and got no response. Then he knocked louder, and soon was pounding on the door as if he intended to break it down. He was stopped by a man shouting from the inside, "We don't want any."

A moment later, Sarah opened the door and let out a stale barroom smell. She carried a beer in one hand but it wasn't necessary because she was already drunk. Dylan was dismayed and disgusted.

"Hey, Dylan," she cried happily. "Hey, look," she called to somebody inside. "It's my sober old surf buddy, Dylan."

Doug came to the door and set his arm across Sarah's shoulder. He was wearing what appeared to be the same jeans and the same Dead Kennedys t-shirt. Dylan felt unclean just looking at him.

Doug smiled with self-satisfaction and said, "Hey, Sobriety Patrol, want a beer? Sorry we started without you, but we didn't know you were coming." He chuckled.

"I can't believe you gave her a drink," Dylan said.

"I didn't give her nothing," Doug said. "She was drunk when I got here."

Sarah giggled as if getting drunk were an accomplishment.

"Is that true?"

Apparently, Sarah didn't like Dylan's tone because she suddenly turned nasty. "I told you I couldn't stay on the wagon alone. But you turned your back on me. What was I supposed to do?"

"I told you what to do," Dylan said. "You didn't listen."

"You're the one who didn't listen. I think you better go now."

Doug took his arm off Sarah's shoulders and let it swing free. Dylan could barely see Sarah behind his bulk. Doug said, "Yeah, Mr. Clean. Scram. Sarah and I like our privacy."

Dylan held out his hand and said, "Come with me, Sarah. I can help you."

Doug bent a little to put his face in Dylan's, and said, "She's not going anywhere." His breath was amazing; Dylan almost passed out from it. It made Dylan angry.

"That's up to her, isn't it?"

"I don't think so," Doug said, and took a swing at Dylan. But he didn't balance very well, and when Dylan sidestepped the punch, Doug almost went over the railing into the pool. Dylan threw him back into the apartment. Doug fell against the coffee table and hit his head. He shook his head, but he didn't get up.

"Come with me, Sarah," Dylan said.

Sarah sat on the floor and cradled Doug's head in her lap. She looked up at Dylan and screamed at him, "Get out. Get out. Get out." She had the face of an animal. Dylan didn't know her. Maybe he'd never known her.

He walked slowly along the balcony to the stairs while Sarah crooned at Doug that everything was going to be all right.

Dylan felt like six tons of mud. In the back of his mind, he heard Ben say, "You work *your* program, Dylan. Let Sarah work *hers.*" Dylan knew you couldn't save people who didn't want to be saved. And yet he could not help feeling guilty. He'd failed her. He could have given her a little more support. On the other hand, there might not be enough support in the world to help Sarah. If she ever came back to the program he might find out.

He drove around for a while, and on an impulse stopped at an all-night coffee shop. He had coffee and a piece of what they called homemade apple pie. The coffee may have been young and strong once, and the pie was mostly sugar and lard. Without finishing, he paid, left too big a tip, and went home to take a shower.

9

Did you ever have to make up your mind?

TIM'S KISS WORRIED BRENDA SO MUCH THAT she barely got any sleep that night. She was awake when her alarm clock went off, but she didn't get up. She just lay there feeling depressed and confused.

Before she met Tim, she had her life organized—at least the love part of it. But the kiss had been really awesome; it was the kind of kiss you wouldn't expect to get from just any guy. If Tim was the love of her life and not Dylan, where did that leave her? If she could be so wrong about Dylan, she feared that she could be wrong about anything.

She lay there for a long time, listening to the house wake up around her, and thinking. Eventually, Brandon came by, dressed and with his books under his arm. He asked her if she was sick.

"I'm sick," Brenda said, "but not from germs."

Brenda sat up and looked at her clock. She plopped her hands into her lap and shook her head at them.

Brandon knew what the problem was, but he didn't understand why it was a big deal. He asked, "It's Tim, isn't it?"

"He drove me home and we were out on the porch talking and he kissed me. Or I kissed him. I'm not sure which."

"Brenda, it was just a kiss."

"Then why do I feel so awful?"

Dylan was one of Brandon's best friends, but Brandon could not make himself angry that Brenda had kissed another guy. He'd seen relationships come and go. If this one survived Tim Matthews, then it was worth saving. If not, then not. It was better to find out earlier than later. He said, "I think we're supposed to kiss a few different people before we settle down with one person for life. You know what they say: You have to kiss a lot of frogs before you find a prince."

"But I was so sure, you know? I was sure that Dylan and I were, like, you know, meant for each other."

"Maybe you are and maybe you're not. Do you have to decide now?"

"Of course not. But why did I do it? What's wrong with me? I liked it. I liked *him*." Brandon had rarely seen his sister looking so beaten.

Brandon said, "Congratulations. On this day in history, Brenda Walsh discovered that she was human."

She stared at him with the long-suffering sarcastic face she used when she didn't want to admit Brandon had scored a point. She said, "Get out of here, Brandon. I have to get ready for school."

Because Brandon didn't like to see Brenda so depressed, he was pleased that he'd managed to prod her out of bed. Once she got moving, she would be all right. She would still have her problem, but it would not overwhelm her as it had when she was in bed with nothing to do but imagine horrible things about herself. He knew that *he* was always less gloomy if somebody could force *him* back into the world of the living.

Down in the kitchen, Brandon found his mom mixing up some hot tea with lemon and honey for his dad. Evidently, all that *karaoke* had finally caught up with him. He made little throat-clearing noises.

While Brandon gnawed on a slice of buttered toast, his mom reacted with dismay to Mr. Walsh's resolve to do scales to strengthen his voice. "Look at Sinatra. Look at Tony Bennett. They're both a lot older than I am, and still going strong."

Brandon didn't have a particular problem with his father's singing, though if he heard "Do Wah

Diddy" one more time, he'd go crazy. As far as Brandon was concerned, the problem was with *karaoke* itself. When the Peach Pit was crowded, the energy was high and any good upbeat song could be entertaining, no matter how wonky the performance. But during slack periods, *karaoke* could be deadly. With some distress, he remembered one afternoon when a woman had insisted on bleating "Your Cheatin' Heart" over and over again until Nat had turned off the power on the machine and told her it was broken.

Brenda came into the kitchen with her books grasped to her chest. She was dressed nicely and looked surprisingly chipper. If her worries of the night had not evaporated, at least she had them under control.

Mrs. Walsh said, "So, Brenda, is there anything you want to tell us?"

Brenda glanced at Brandon, and they shared a moment of sibling pain and understanding. "About what?" Brenda asked. She began to calmly peel an orange.

Brandon knew what Mom was getting to, just as Brenda must. It was certainly the last thing Brenda wanted to talk about to a parent.

"Well, for what it's worth, I liked your friend Tim."

That was a big mistake, Brandon thought; Mom's comment would have exactly the opposite effect from the one she desired. As far as Brenda would be concerned, a parent liking a boyfriend was the kiss of death.

Mr. Walsh put a stake through the heart of Brenda's relationship with Tim by saying, "Yeah. He told me he's premed at UCLA. A nice hard-working kid."

Brenda was now tearing peel off the orange and flinging the bits onto the table. She said, "Yes, Dad, he's a solid citizen. Exactly the type of boy parents swoon over."

"Well, I think he's very nice," Mrs. Walsh said with conviction, as if somebody had been arguing with her.

Brenda said, "What are you saying, exactly? That you want me to go out with someone 'nice' like Tim instead of someone wild and crazy like Dylan?"

Brandon could see by the startled look in his mom's eyes, that she understood at last what she had done. "No, honey. We love Dylan. You know that. But you're young yet. You have plenty of time to meet nice people."

"What we're saying," Mr. Walsh said, "is that we'd certainly understand if you decided you wanted to date other guys."

"Who I date is my business," Brenda said angrily. She left the peeled orange on the table, quickly rinsed the juice off her fingers under the tap and stomped out of the room with her books.

Mrs. Walsh glared at her husband. He said, "I was just trying to be considerate."

"Dad," Brandon said, "what Brenda wants at the moment is not consideration but answers."

"To what?" Mrs. Walsh asked.

Brandon had trapped himself. Brenda's problem was not exactly a secret, but he didn't feel right discussing it with his parents either. Brandon said, "You know: life, the universe, and everything."

"That's pretty vague," Mr. Walsh said.

Brandon had to agree. After a moment, he told them the least he decided he could get away with. "You may understand if Brenda dates other guys, but she doesn't." While his parents thought about his statement, he grabbed his books, gave them a jolly good-bye, and made a tactical retreat.

Brandon found Brenda waiting for him out by the Mustang. She asked, "What did you tell them?"

"What makes you think I told them anything?"

"My exit was a little abrupt. They'd ask you questions. You'd have to answer. What do you tell them?"

Brandon nodded at Brenda's analysis. He would have figured it the same way. He said, "I told them that dating can be a lot of work."

"That's all?"

"Pretty much. Look, do you want a sworn statement or do you want to get to school on time?"

Brenda submitted to getting into the car. The drive to school would have been frostier, but Brenda spent most of it looking out the window, wondering, Brandon supposed, what she would do about Tim and Dylan.

After school, Brandon went to work at the Peach Pit. Some guy was on the *karaoke* singing a not very tuneful version of "That Old Black Magic." The few other customers paid him no attention, but he was in a dream world of his own and didn't notice.

Shortly, Steve, Andrea, David, and Donna came in. Their faces curled up when they saw the Sinatra impersonator, but they settled into a booth anyway. Brandon gave them a few minutes to decide what they wanted—during which an unusual amount of discussion seemed to be going on—and then went to take their orders.

The old guy finished "That Old Black Magic," and the silence was blessed. Brandon stood there with his pencil poised over his pad just listening. He hadn't realized how difficult listening to that guy had been until the guy stopped. The customers seemed to enjoy the silence, too, for their faces relaxed, and they began to talk among themselves. Brandon was about to ask his friends what they would have when the old guy started in on "My Way."

Steve said, "We have to talk."

"Sounds serious," Brandon said. He suspected what the subject would be but waited for them to spring it on him.

"You bet," David said. "We can't take it any more."

"The noise pollution," Andrea explained.

"He's doing it his way," Donna said.

Brandon turned, and with his friends watched the old man sing. The man was oblivious to every-thing but the song. Brandon turned back to his friends and said, "I thought you guys liked *karaoke*."

Steve said, "Too much of a good thing, Brandon. This place is turning into a Las Vegas lounge. A third-rate Las Vegas lounge."

"It's like the Peach Pit isn't ours anymore," Donna said. "Can we order now?"

Brandon nodded and said, "Great minds think alike. I'll talk to Nat."

"You tell him, Brandon," Steve said. "Either *karaoke* goes or we go."

It was like Steve to unnecessarily push a request into a threat: he thought of himself as a tough guy and a wheeler-dealer. But Steve and the others were right. *Karaoke* had to go or the Pit was doomed.

Nat was standing at the cash register contemplating the *karaoke* stage and the guy singing "My Way." He was drumming his fingers nervously on the little rubber mat next to the register, but not in time with the music.

Brandon walked up next to him and said, "Nat, we have a problem."

Without taking his eyes off the singer, Nat said, "What's that?"

"It's *karaoke*, Nat. The Peach Pit isn't the same since you brought it in here."

"That's for sure."

Brandon was surprised by Nat's response. He thought that Nat was still high on *karaoke*, and that he'd have a hell of a time talking Nat into dropping it. Evidently, that would not be the case.

Thus encouraged, Brandon said, "My friends

are saying that if you don't do something about the floor show, they'll boycott."

"I don't blame them." He looked at Brandon and went on, "*Karaoke* is great, but the Peach Pit's a juke joint. It always has been and always will be."

"What about the money?"

Nat shrugged. "You kids are the life's blood of this place. Without you, the Pit's just another burger palace."

"Then you'll take it out?"

"As soon as I can," Nat said. "But you have to do one thing for me, Brandon."

This entire conversation had gone much better than Brandon had supposed it would. "Sure, Nat, anything."

"You have to be the one who delivers the big news to your father."

Brandon's optimistic attitude collapsed. His dad had never been to the Peach Pit during the day and so could not know how dreadful *karaoke* could be if the wrong singer got possession of the microphone. He hoped his dad would not take the news too hard, but Brandon feared the worst.

For the rest of the day, Brandon went over in his head what he might say to his father, but he did not come up with an approach he liked. Quitting time came, and he changed into his street clothes. Nat caught him as he was heading for the door.

"You have to tell him tonight, Brandon. After closing I'm going to pack everything up, and tomorrow there'll be an ad in the classifieds."

Brandon nodded. He would have liked more time to come up with the right words, but maybe just leaping in was the best method.

10

Pick up on one and leave the other behind

BRANDON DROVE HOME FROM THE PEACH Pit still considering first one approach and then another. He had not yet come to a decision when he found Mr. Walsh in the living room reading the paper.

Brandon sat down at the opposite end of the couch and said, "Dad, I have to talk to you."

Mr. Walsh rattled the paper in half and looked at Brandon worriedly. Brandon had obviously begun badly. The guy thought he was about to admit he was taking drugs or something. Brandon would have to lighten up.

"We're having a little problem down at the Peach Pit."

"Really? What's that?" Dad still seemed concerned. He liked to solve problems—he considered them a challenge.

"Nat's customers are trickling away. He's losing money."

"Do you know what's causing this loss of business?"

"We do, but Nat's afraid to change anything. He doesn't want to hurt anybody's feelings."

Mr. Walsh shook his head. "Nat's running a business, not a charity. Whatever it is has to go. What is it?"

Dad seemed so innocent that Brandon almost didn't tell him. But he hated to think of his father driving down to the Peach Pit to use a *karaoke* setup that was no longer there. Besides, Mr. Walsh would rightfully and righteously demand to know why he hadn't been told that his great experiment had failed.

Brandon said, "It's the *karaoke*."

"What?"

"It's the *karaoke*, Dad. If you could see the lounge acts the customers are sometimes assaulted by, you'd understand. A lot of Nat's regulars are threatening to stop coming in."

Mr. Walsh seemed embarrassed. He said, "I see," and began to neaten up his newspaper. "How does Nat feel about this?"

"He's grateful for your help, Dad, but he's ready to

admit that *karaoke* is just not working out. Tomorrow he plugs in the jukebox again."

Mr. Walsh sighed. "It seemed like a good idea."

"It was a good idea, Dad. The novelty just wore off."

"Yeah," Mr. Walsh said with regret.

Brandon left his father sitting next to his neatly folded newspaper and staring into space. A few hours later, Mrs. Walsh came into Brandon's room and reported that Mr. Walsh had taken his electric organ from the closet and was accompanying himself as he sang "Wild Thing." No one could hear the music but Mr. Walsh. With the bedroom door closed, no one could hear Mr. Walsh.

"Thank goodness for headphones," Mrs. Walsh said.

"Amen to that, Mom," Brandon said.

Brenda was leery of going back to cardio-funk class because she did not want to run into Tim. But she finally went because she needed the workout. She couldn't allow Tim to run her life, not even indirectly.

Tim was there, but he said nothing either to her or Kelly during class. Brenda tried to get into the music and the movement, and did succeed in losing herself a few times. But between routines, while catching her breath, she saw Tim on the other side of the room. The thought of the inevitable confrontation made her sweat in a way that had nothing to do with the exercise she was getting.

When class was over, he approached her and Kelly. He seemed in a pleasant enough mood, but that would not help Brenda do what she had to do. As a matter of fact, Tim's disposition would only make things more difficult. Brenda's first impulse was to run, but she couldn't do that. She was a Walsh, and she had had drummed into her that she had to face her responsibilities.

Kelly backed off to a discreet distance—far enough away to give them some privacy but close enough to hear everything.

Evidently Tim saw from Brenda's expression what she had in mind because he said, "Okay. Lay it on me."

"I'm sorry," Brenda said. "We shouldn't see each other again." She found, much to her surprise and pleasure, that she was not as sorry as she had supposed she would be.

"Why not? You're only in high school. You should be going out with lots of guys." He was pleasant but forceful.

"I don't want to. I want to go out with Dylan."

"But he hung you out to dry last night."

"Not really. He left because someone needed him." Having said that, Brenda realized that she understood Dylan for the first time, and she admired him and loved him even more.

"I'm sorry," said Tim. "I jumped to conclusions."

"That's okay."

"I guess I just wanted to believe that Dylan was some kind of creep. I hope he appreciates you."

"I think he does." Then Brenda thought of something else she could say. It was from *Casablanca*, one of the old movies that Dylan was always taking her to. She punched Tim in the shoulder and said, "'Here's looking at *you*, kid,'" leaving him astonished.

Brenda walked toward the locker room, feeling that she had done her difficult job well. She turned at the door to see where Kelly was, and observed Tim engaging her in conversation. Kelly laughed. Brenda approved of their getting together. Tim was a nice guy. Maybe he and Kelly were right for each other.

Brenda had a powerful need to speak with Dylan. She was certain that she was right for Dylan, and she'd dumped a nice guy like Tim on the strength of her feelings. Her only question now was whether Dylan felt that he was right for her. After all, she still had no idea how he really felt about that Sarah person. She had to know.

That evening she went over to his house. He was there watching a surfing video that he immediately shut off with the remote as she entered the living room. They sat on the couch without touching. They could not touch yet, not until Brenda knew where she stood.

They spoke about *karaoke,* about surfing, about cardio-funk, about anything except what was really on their minds. And then Dylan said, "I know the past few days have been hard on you, Bren, but this girl, Sarah, really needed me."

One of the things Brenda liked about Dylan was

his sensitivity, but she still didn't have the answers she needed. "I know AA's a big part of your life, but you heard what Ben said about letting each person work his or her own program."

Dylan rested his hand on the open space between them. He shrugged and said, "Well, as it turned out, Sarah didn't want my help anyway. Last I saw of her, she and her boyfriend were curled up with a bottle."

"I'm sorry." She really was sorry, but she could not help being aware that Sarah's defects made it easier to get back together with Dylan.

"It's strange." Dylan seemed to be explaining to himself as much as to Brenda. "I know that you can't save somebody who doesn't want to be saved. Hell, I was that somebody myself for a long time. But when you see somebody drowning—"

"I know. It breaks your heart."

There was a long silence, but it was comfortable. Brenda, at any rate, was thinking about how easy it was to go a little crazy, and then justify that craziness.

Dylan asked, "So, do I need to worry about this cardio-funk guy?"

"No. Not anymore." She moved her hand across the open space to touch his. He put his hand over hers. It felt good. She pulled her hand away suddenly, causing him to look at her with surprise. "Dylan, I kissed him."

Dylan did not seem bothered. "It happens," he said.

"Did it happen to you?"

A moment later, he admitted that it had.

They were even, then. Each of them had had a little fling, but neither fling had lasted. Dylan's admission stopped her from feeling guilty, but Brenda was still fearful. What if Sarah had been a reformed drunk instead of a drunk? What if Tim showed up again? Anything could happen. She said, "Dylan, what's wrong with us?"

"Maybe nothing," Dylan said. "Nothing unusual, anyway. It must happen all the time that somebody catches the eye of somebody else who's already spoken for. But if you're in love, you're flattered and then you find the strength to look the other way."

Brenda moved closer to Dylan. They hugged. She said, "I don't want something like this to split us up."

"Me neither," said Dylan. "Not just before Valentine's Day, anyway."

She pulled back to look at him. "Oh, you!" Brenda cried. "What has Valentine's Day got to do with it?"

"I went to a lot of trouble to set up an intimate experience for the two of us."

"What sort of intimate experience?"

"You'll see."

"Tell me, you bum."

"You'll see," Dylan said again.

11

Secrets that pass in the night

BRENDA TRIED NOT TO WORRY ABOUT THE random factors that could suddenly change a person's life, but at odd moments thoughts about Sarah and Tim came back to her. Andrea Zuckerman called what happened when these sudden changes occurred "being shafted by existential doom." Brenda was not sure what that meant, but the phrase had the proper thunderous sound to describe enormous but unpredictable events.

With Valentine's Day approaching, Brenda had other things on her mind, like the surprise plans Dylan had made for the two of them. He refused to tell her what they were. And his clues might describe anything from going bowling to reading the encyclopedia.

"Give it a rest, Bren," Dylan had said. "If I tell you, it'll be like opening your Christmas presents before Christmas."

Brenda agreed with Dylan, but she could not prevent herself from being curious, so almost against her will, she kept at him. His latest clue was that they would be lying down.

"Sounds sexy," Donna had commented.

Kelly had said nothing, though she was standing right there and heard everything. Lately, she seemed moody and preoccupied, and had a tendency to snap at people for no reason.

Donna, however, was enthusiastic about Valentine's Day. Suddenly, it had become her favorite holiday, probably because she had a boyfriend now, even if it was only David Silver. David had grown up a lot in the past year or so, and was not nearly the geek he'd been when the Walshes had first come to town from Minnesota. At one time, David had had a remarkable crush on Kelly, and now, David's dad was going with Kelly's mom and they were nearly related. Amazing! More existential doom.

Brenda marched through the crowded halls of West Beverly High with Kelly and Donna. Donna bubbled with stories of the cute things David had done, and Kelly was somber, as had become her habit.

They stopped at the corner where the school DJ booth was located. Nobody was in there at the moment, but Brenda could look right in through the glass and see all the equipment, records, and CDs. Brenda, Kelly, and Donna frequently used that corner as a meeting place because David Silver was the most popular DJ at West Beverly and he spent a lot of time in the booth. Which meant, of course, that Donna spent a lot of time swooning over him there.

Hoping to draw her out, Brenda asked Kelly, "What do you think Dylan has planned for Valentine's?"

"I have a flash for you, Brenda. Not only do I not know, but I don't care."

"Excuse me for living," Brenda said. Kelly was a good friend, but her grumpiness was getting tiresome. Donna rolled her eyes, evidently agreeing with Brenda.

David walked up wearing his usual expression of barely controlled enthusiasm. He said hello to Kelly and Brenda, and gave Donna a peck on the cheek. He said, "Listen, Kelly, about Valentine's Day: my dad and I are coming over to your place for dinner, and I was wondering—since it is Valentine's Day and all—if I could bring Donna?"

To Brenda that seemed like a reasonable request, and Donna looked hopeful, but Kelly said, "No, it's not okay."

Brenda was surprised. Donna and David looked as if each of them had been hit on the back of the head with a mallet.

"Sorry," David said. "I didn't realize I was asking for the moon."

"What is your problem, Kelly?" Donna asked angrily.

"I'm not even sure there will be a dinner," Kelly said.

David smiled and said, "I guess we're on our own then."

"Good." Donna looked at Kelly when she spoke.

"I'm glad that's settled," David said. "I have to start my show." He kissed Donna again, and stepped into the DJ booth.

Brenda knew they would be late for their next class if they didn't get moving. She walked down the hall, and as she had hoped, Kelly and Donna followed, more out of habit than anything else.

Donna said, "You know, Kelly, I'm getting pretty tired of you being so mean to David all the time for no reason."

"I don't want to talk about it," Kelly said.

"Come on, Kelly," Brenda said. "If something's wrong, you can tell us. We're your best friends."

Donna said, "If you can't trust us, who can you trust?"

Kelly looked at them with big worried eyes. Apparently, whatever it was concerned Kelly a great deal. She made them swear a bloody oath that they would not repeat to anybody the secret they were about to hear. Then she said, "I can't believe this is happening."

"What?" Brenda asked.

Kelly said, "They're always after us to be careful, and now—"

"No," said Brenda with astonishment. She knew what Kelly was beating around the bush about.

"Oh yes," Kelly said and nodded.

"What?" Donna cried.

Kelly took Donna's arm and said, "My mom is pregnant."

"It can't be," Donna said. "Can it?"

"Mom took every home test in the drug store, and they all say that it can. Then she went to the doctor and she agreed. There is no doubt."

"Does your Mom want more children?" Donna asked.

"I don't think so."

"What about Mel?" Brenda asked.

"Mom's convinced that he doesn't want any more either."

Brenda said, "Then what's the problem? Do what needs to be done."

"That's the scary part," Kelly said. "Mom isn't sure she wants to."

"This is too weird," Donna said.

"Sounds to me," Brenda said, "as if you are about to get a job as a permanent in-house baby-sitter."

"Yeah," Kelly said unhappily.

David Silver did a live public service announcement, and then punched up the next record. He could see Donna outside the studio, eager to come in. Her eagerness was one of the things David found endearing. She was kind of a chucklehead, but David loved her. He switched off the mike, the ON THE AIR sign went off, and Donna entered the studio, a little breathless and excited.

This whole business with Kelly was unpleasant, but he understood perfectly why she was always nasty to him. He'd had a mad crush on her the year before, and she had done her best to ignore him. Now, he was in her face all the time because her mom and his dad were so tight.

As far as Donna's presence at Valentine's dinner was concerned, David didn't understand Kelly's attitude at all. David was used to Kelly's rudeness being directed at him, but Donna was an unusual target. Donna was simpatico—not only David's main squeeze, but one of Kelly's best friends. Maybe Kelly was just nervous because she'd guessed what was going to happen.

Donna threw herself into a chair and said, "I must talk to you."

"Me, too. I know why Kelly's been acting so weird. She must sense that something is up."

Donna nodded as if she understood, and then worriedly asked, "Up?"

David made sure the mike was closed, and then asked, "Can you keep a secret?"

"Of course."

That did not reassure David. Donna was honest and certainly believed what she said, but she was also a great blurter. Secrets were known to escape

Donna merely because of the enthusiasm David otherwise so admired. Still, having asked the question, keeping the secret from her would be very difficult. Hoping for the best, he said, "Check it out: My dad told me that he's planning to propose to Kelly's mom on Valentine's Day."

David's revelation seemed to please Donna. She said, "That's so romantic. Especially under the circumstances."

"What circumstances?"

"The baby, of course."

Donna was not the best straight-line thinker in the world, but she generally got her facts right.

"What baby?" David asked.

Donna stood up stiffly and knotted her fingers together. She looked horrified, which further served to confuse David. She said, "I can't tell you. I promised. Kelly would kill me."

"You can't leave me hanging, Donna. Besides, I'm your boyfriend. Besides, if there's a baby involved, I ought to know. You must tell me."

"I'll tell you. But you must never tell anybody where you heard it."

"On my honor." He held up two fingers in the Cub Scout salute.

Donna blurted out, "Kelly's mom is pregnant. That must be why your dad is proposing marriage."

David's mind spun with ideas. "That can't be true. My dad would have told me."

Donna looked uncomfortable.

"What? There's more?"

"David, what if your dad doesn't know?"

David considered this new idea. If his dad didn't know, then it was okay he hadn't told him. But if his dad didn't know, wasn't it David's responsibility to tell him? Not necessarily. After all, it wasn't David's baby. And he had promised Donna not to tell anyone. Sheesh, this was tangled. He could begin by finding out if his dad knew or not. That seemed to be fairly safe.

David said, "Listen to me, Donna. This conversation never took place. You didn't tell me anything and I don't know anything. We're back to the beginning. Got it?"

"No problem," Donna said. She sat down again, apparently relieved. A moment later, she began to browse through the library of singles.

David hoped she was right to believe that their conversation would remain a secret, but it seemed unlikely that any of them would get off so easy.

That afternoon when school was out, David drove over to Century City to see his father at his office. Two sorrowful people were in the waiting room when he came in. They looked up at him to have something new to look at.

Arlene, Dad's receptionist, had known David since he was a baby. She always made a comment about how nice he looked or how much he'd grown. When he was a kid, David was pleased to believe everything she said. But in the past few years, David found it increasingly difficult to figure out whether Arlene really believed the stuff she said, or whether she said it only to make David feel good. Her compliments rarely pleased David these days; they rankled him a little because they meant Arlene thought he was vain. When the ceremonial greetings were over, Arlene told David to go right in.

David found his dad studying an X-ray of some teeth. "Hey, Dad."

Dr. Silver clipped the X-ray to a light panel and said with delight, "David! What a pleasant surprise. To what do I owe?"

"Just checking in, Dad. Making sure everything is all right." David wasn't lying, but he felt as if he were not being entirely straight either. He hated this roundabout questioning, but other than admitting what he knew, he saw no other course to take.

"Couldn't be better. Have a look at this." Dr. Silver pulled a small velvet box from the pocket of his white smock and invited David to open it. Inside was an enormous diamond ring.

Trying to sound enthusiastic, David said, "Wow."

"It cost a fortune, but what the hell, if anyone is worth it, Jackie is."

David nodded. Jackie was Kelly's mom. At least that part was working out okay. David said, "I guess that's it for big big news."

Dr. Silver put the ring away and regarded David seriously. "Is something wrong, son?"

"I don't know. Should there be?" He smiled.

Dr. Silver put his hand on David's shoulder and said, "I know this change in our lives can't be easy for you, but remember that I'm always here for you first and foremost. You can always talk to your old dad."

"I appreciate that. I just wanted to make sure you were all right."

Dr. Silver looked confused, which seemed only fair, David being a little confused himself.

Dr. Silver said, "David, this is what I want. Jackie is making me very happy."

His dad didn't know about the baby, David was sure of it. There was no reason for his dad to keep it a secret. Of course, David was not entirely clear why Jackie Taylor wanted to keep it a secret.

David wondered again if he should tell his dad everything he knew. But telling would not only incriminate Donna, it would also complicate the situation for his dad. If he really didn't know about the baby—which seemed likely—he would have to go on pretending he didn't know. Yet, didn't his dad have a right to know that the woman he intended to marry was pregnant?

David could see that by saying nothing, he'd made a decision, but he could not see anything else to do.

David submitted to a hug from his dad and to more meaningless compliments from Arlene, and escaped as quickly as possible. Short of screwing things up further, he'd done everything he could. The best thing he could do now was just hunker down and lay low. He didn't want to have his head up when the shooting started.

12

Indecent proposal

DOWN AT THE PEACH PIT, BRANDON TAPED the final paper heart to the wall and stood back to survey his handiwork. As usual, Nat had insisted on making a big deal over the holiday. He'd ordered Brandon to put up cupids and hearts all over the place. The effect was not subtle, but no one could deny that it was seasonal. Nat put his approval on the job and went back to work behind the counter.

Being at loose ends romantically at the moment, Brandon was indifferent to Valentine's Day. As far as he was concerned, it was just another excuse to sell greeting cards.

In one of the booths, Steve was brooding about whether he should send Kelly a Valentine's card. They had been a very hot couple until Kelly dropped him. Steve never could quite accept the fact that their romance was over. Because they remained friends and saw each other every day at school, Steve had an even more difficult time; he spent his days alternately scheming how to get Kelly back, and proclaiming that he wouldn't have her back if she came to him on her hands and knees.

At one end of the counter, Andrea was marveling over Nat's racing form. While she slowly turned the pages, Nat said, "It's the one and only paper that gives true meaning to the words, 'news you can use.'"

"You can actually read this?" Andrea asked. Brandon looked over her shoulder at column after column of tiny words and numbers.

"Sure I can read it," Nat said. He took one side of the page Andrea was looking at and pointed out the features. "See here, these are all the horses on today's card at the track. It tells you the horse, the owner, the trainer, the jockey, and how each horse did in his past few races."

"Do you need a code book?" Brandon asked.

"What?" Both Nat and Andrea were surprised by Brandon's question.

"Never mind," said Brandon. "It's a gag in an old Marx Brothers' movie. You see, Chico sells Groucho a hot tip, but Groucho can't use it till he has all these code books and guides and stuff that Chico keeps selling him."

Nat said, "This isn't the movies, Brandon. This is serious business. You see, Andrea, the racing form tells you everything you need to know to make an informed selection. Or . . ." He took the paper from Andrea, folded it, and flung it down the counter. "Or you can forget about the statistics and just pick a winner out of thin air."

Andrea reached for the form and opened it. "Since none of this makes any sense to me, I'll try the 'thin air' approach."

"What's going on?" Steve asked. He'd snuck up on them while they were looking at the paper.

"Quiet," Brandon said. "Andrea's picking a horse." He, Nat, and Steve watched Andrea with tolerant good humor.

Andrea said, "I like this one: the three horse in the eighth race."

"Why?" Brandon asked. "I'm just curious, you understand."

Andrea shrugged. "I just like its name."

Sarcastically, Steve said, "You don't pick a horse by its name, Andrea."

"I just have a feeling, then, okay?"

Nat had been watching Andrea with increasing interest. As she spoke, his smile faded to be replaced by an expression of hope and wild suspicion.

Brandon said, "Tell her, Nat: Horse racing is not a guessing game. It's a statistical science."

"Normally it's a science," Nat said. "But I once had a girlfriend who used to do the same thing. She just picked a horse she felt good about."

"How'd she do?" Steve asked.

Nat shook his head. "Came up a winner every time. Of course, I never listened to her. Maybe that's why we broke up."

"Trust me, Nat," Andrea said. "Number three in the eighth."

While Nat speculated on Andrea's reliability, Brandon asked, "What's the name of that horse, anyway?"

Andrea blushed and said, "Lovesick."

Brandon didn't like the sound of that. He and Andrea had been friends since he'd joined the staff of the *West Beverly Blaze*, and for almost that long, Andrea had been trying to make their friendship something more. He could not convince himself that the name of Andrea's horse did not have some special meaning for her.

When Brandon's shift was over, he found Nat sitting at the counter staring at the racing form with a tormented look on his face.

"Lovesick?" Brandon asked.

"Who knows? Good night, Brandon."

"Good night, Nat."

On his drive home, Brandon wondered how long he would have a job. Like a lot of people, Nat didn't think about money much if he had enough of it. But Nat's new preoccupation with making money—first with *karaoke* and now with Andrea's horse-predicting talents—was not a good sign. Brandon would not be the first employee who was laid off because his employer could no longer afford the luxury of having him around.

The family gathered for dinner. Brenda looked as if she were excited about something, but it wasn't until they were all seated and had meat on their plates that she said, "So, what would you say if I told you that a certain mother of a certain friend of ours, who's going out with a certain father of a certain other friend of ours, is pregnant."

"Who?" Brandon asked, only moderately interested. He hated it when Brenda acted coy.

"Take a wild guess," Brenda suggested.

"Jackie and Mel?" Mrs. Walsh asked.

"You didn't hear it from me," Brenda said.

They all looked at her with astonishment. They'd all known that they were going together and, being a modern couple, Jackie and Mel would certainly have been intimate. Still, Brandon would have thought that Jackie and Mel were done having kids and would have taken the proper precautions.

Mr. Walsh said, "Is that a good idea? I mean, Jackie's got to be pushing forty."

"She's been pushing it for a while, Dad," Brenda said. "Kelly's freaking."

"I'd freak, too, if Mom got pregnant," Brandon said.

"Not me. I'd like it," Brenda said.

"Sure," said Brandon, "until you had to change a diaper in the middle of the night. Or until you had to baby-sit instead of going on a date."

Mrs. Walsh said, "Maybe I should give Jackie a call."

"Please don't, Mom. It's supposed to be a secret. Kelly made me swear."

Brandon was disgusted. Brenda couldn't keep a secret any more than a sieve could hold water. He said, "So you came right home and told us?"

"I didn't tell. Mom guessed."

"Right." The human capacity for self-delusion was infinite.

Mr. and Mrs. Walsh continued to discuss what it might be like to have a baby at their age. Mr. Walsh was generally against it, but Mrs. Walsh got all dreamy-eyed thinking about having a new rug rat in the house.

It wasn't long before Brenda had had enough, and she attempted to change the subject. "So," she said to Brandon, "did Dylan tell you what he and I are doing for Valentine's?"

"No, what?"

"I thought he might have told you."

"Maybe he did. But when one of *my* friends tells me a secret, my lips are sealed."

"It's not the same thing at all," Brenda said, though she knew it was. A secret should be a sacred trust.

She prodded Brandon some more, but he refused to tell her anything. He even refused to give her a clue.

"You don't know," she said.

"Probably not," Brandon said, and smiled.

"Brandon!"

Brenda didn't learn anything about Valentine's

Day, but at least they were no longer talking about babies.

Kelly Taylor was outraged that Donna had told David Silver about the baby. It was true that Donna had at least had the gumption and honesty to come over and report what she'd done, but that didn't excuse her. Kelly felt that she would never again be able to trust Donna. They were in Kelly's room. Mrs. Taylor did not yet know what had happened.

"It just slipped out," Donna cried for about the hundredth time.

"Evidently swearing a bloody oath means nothing to you."

"It does, Kelly. It really does. But when David told me his dad was going to ask your mom to marry him, I just assumed—"

"What?" Kelly was so astonished, she wasn't sure she'd heard Donna correctly.

Donna seemed reticent to repeat herself, so Kelly had to ask, "David's father wants to propose to my mother?"

Donna nodded miserably, and said, "He wants to do it at dinner on Valentine's Day."

The situation was becoming too complicated and unpleasant for Kelly to bear. She now knew a secret at least as earth-shattering as the one concerning the baby. There was no telling how her mom would react to it if she knew. Of course, Kelly had never sworn that she would not tell about the proposal, so she could tell without anybody accusing her of breaking a bloody oath. But knowing that telling was possible, and deciding that telling was a good idea were two different things.

Donna watched Kelly with growing apprehension. At last, she said, "I know I shouldn't have said anything, but you'll see. Everybody will live happily ever after. I promise."

Kelly doubted whether Donna's promise meant anything in this case, but she pretended to be mollified just to get rid of her. The damage had already been done. All of Donna's apologies could not change that. Now, it was up to Kelly to figure out what to do about it.

Painting her toenails always relaxed her because she had to concentrate so hard on doing it right. She got out some polish in a color called Fireapple Red and began. About halfway through her second foot, she decided that all of this secretiveness was the root of the problem. It was ridiculous. If everybody would only sit down and discuss the situation openly, everybody's nerves would be better off.

She marched into her mom's bedroom, where Kelly found her propped up in bed with pillows, casually flipping through *Good Housekeeping*, a magazine that had not interested Mrs. Taylor since Kelly had been a child. Kelly feared that her mom really would keep the baby. That could only make the situation more complicated, regardless of who knew what.

"How's Donna?" Mrs. Taylor asked.

"Fine," Kelly said. She sat on the edge of her mom's bed and wondered where to begin.

Mrs. Taylor put down the magazine and asked, "Something wrong?"

"Wrong? No. Not wrong. Not exactly."

Mrs. Taylor turned over the magazine on her knees and said, "What is it exactly, then? You look awful."

Kelly said, "David Silver knows that you're pregnant."

Mrs. Taylor looked at her, dumbfounded. After a moment, she said, "How?"

Without looking at her mom, Kelly told the entire story about Donna and David. There was no point holding anything back. She felt so guilty about having told Donna and Brenda about the baby that Kelly was determined to fix everything even if it meant getting chewed out by her mom and being grounded till she was on Social Security.

Mrs. Taylor's shock quickly turned to anger. She allowed Kelly to finish, and then began a tirade about trust and responsibility. She said, "I never expected Mel to hear about my pregnancy through the West Beverly High School grapevine." Kelly had not heard a lecture on this subject for many years, and even the shrill and frustrated tone in which it was delivered seemed a relic of her childhood. She felt terrible.

As her mother went on, it occurred to Kelly that considering what she had in the oven, her mother had a lot of nerve accusing her of irresponsibility.

Mrs. Taylor's mistake did not excuse Kelly's own lack of judgment, but Kelly felt justified in fighting back just a little.

She said, "Mother, please. Just because Donna told David doesn't mean that David told Mel."

"Why should I assume that David Silver is any more responsible than my daughter?"

Kelly waited for her mother to continue, but evidently Mrs. Taylor had talked herself out for the moment. She picked up the magazine and threw it down. Kelly decided that she might as well get the whole thing over with now. Forlornly, Kelly said, "I haven't told you everything."

Evidently, Mrs. Taylor was beyond shock. She nodded and said sarcastically, "Of course not. Not satisfied revealing *my* secrets, perhaps you are about to reveal somebody else's?"

Her mom was right of course, which only served to make Kelly feel worse. But she'd started so she had to go on. She said, "Actually, I am. But you'll like it. Really." Kelly hoped that she was right, but there was only one way to find out. She said, "Mom, David told Donna that at Valentine's dinner Mel plans to ask you to marry him. You know, sort of as a Valentine's Day present."

Mrs. Taylor's reaction took Kelly completely by surprise. For some reason, Mrs. Taylor seemed even more horrified by Mel Silver's proposal than she had been by Kelly's security leak.

"What's the matter?" Kelly asked. "Isn't this what you want?"

Mrs. Taylor shook her head and said with disgust, "Of course not. Don't you see? Mel's only asking me to marry him because he feels he has to, not because he loves me."

"That's ridiculous."

"You say that only because you don't know him like I do."

It was ridiculous, but her mom might be right. After all, nobody had acted rationally so far. Why should Dr. Silver be any different?

Mrs. Taylor's anger suddenly evaporated, leaving behind a residue of cold determination. Mrs. Taylor said, "Don't you worry about a thing, honey. This is all my fault. I never should have told you about the baby in the first place. I got myself into this, and now I'm going to get myself out of it. Tomorrow." She picked up the magazine and smiled grimly as she turned the pages.

"Are you okay, Mom?" Kelly asked.

"I'm fine. You'd better get to bed. It's a school night."

"What are you going to do?"

"Let me worry about that. Good night, dear."

Kelly walked back to her bedroom feeling as if she'd just armed a bomb.

13

You bet your life

THE MORE DYLAN TOLD HER, THE LESS Brenda knew about what the two of them were doing for Valentine's Day. She was going crazy. Brandon had told her at last that what Dylan had in mind was very romantic, which Brenda could have guessed, so that was no help.

She and Dylan were sitting in the kitchen drinking coffee and eating homemade cookies. Everyone else was out and they had the house to themselves. Still, Brenda was not in a mood to neck. The truth was, she was a little miffed that Dylan was being so secretive. If she had time to prepare, she could be happy with almost anything, but Dylan refused to cooperate. Part of her was afraid that come Valentine's Day she would be disappointed.

"Okay," Dylan said. "Here's another clue. It's red and it's warm."

Brenda could think of only one thing that might be red and warm. If this was Dylan's idea of romance, maybe she was better off with her fantasies. With some astonishment, she asked, "You got me a sweater?"

"Give me some credit, will you, Bren? No, it's something much more intimate than a sweater."

"Something in red flannel from Trashy Lingerie?"

Dylan smiled as he considered Brenda's guess. "Very funny but incorrect. It's something very close to your heart."

Brenda added up the latest clues. Their Valentine's Day activity was warm, red, and close to her heart. "I don't get it."

"Good."

"Dylan!"

"Have another cookie," Dylan said, and stuck one into Brenda's mouth. She had the satisfaction of knowing that at least Dylan wasn't giving her a sweater.

After school, Brandon and Steve went over to the Peach Pit for life-giving milk shakes. The place was jumping as it usually was after school, but Nat took time out from serving orders to give them each a big welcome.

He shook hands with Brandon and said, "Your girlfriend's horse came in."

"She's not my girlfriend," Brandon said.

"Yeah," said Nat, "well maybe you should reconsider."

Looking a little confused, Steve said, "Wait a minute, Nat. Are you saying that Lovesick won that race?"

"Absolutely. And at fifteen to one."

"And you put money on it?"

"Steve, when opportunity knocks you have to answer the door."

Nat lost interest in them entirely when Andrea entered. He called her Lady Luck, and offered her anything she wanted, on the house.

Brandon felt really weird about this, as if the Peach Pit had suddenly become the Twilight Zone. Though he did not deny that such coincidences could happen, picking the right horse by the patented "thin air" method on the first try seemed so unlikely as to be impossible—like a troop of monkeys typing out Shakespeare's plays without first typing gibberish for centuries. Yet it had happened. Brandon did not begrudge Nat his money nor Andrea her free meal, but he knew it was a mistake to attribute Andrea with a wild talent. It could lead only to trouble, he was certain.

Andrea decided to take advantage of Nat's offer and blow her diet for the week. She had a megaburger, an order of rings, and a strawberry shake. Nat went back to the kitchen to fill her order, and then watched her through the window while he cooked.

Judging by the expression on Nat's face, Brandon was sure he was not just admiring Andrea's good looks. He was a man trying to decide if he could outsmart the fates again by purchasing another pig in a poke. Brandon was not superstitious, but he knew that a person could not persist in going one-on-one with the universe and expect to win very often.

Andrea didn't notice Nat's scrutiny because Steve was distracting her. "So, Andrea," said Steve, "got any particular feelings about the state lottery?"

"Sorry, Steve, I do only horses."

"Can I rub your forehead for luck?"

Andrea looked shocked, and Brandon said, "Don't let's get carried away, Steve."

Nat brought Andrea her food, and allowed her to eat in peace for a few minutes. Brandon could see he was anxious about something, and at last Nat could stand waiting no longer. He went into the back room and come out with the racing form. He stood it up against a catsup bottle in front of Andrea and said, "Do it again."

"Do what again? The business with the horses? That was just dumb luck."

"That's what I'm counting on," Nat said seriously.

Brandon had a bad feeling. Nat was conning himself. "Are you sure about this, Nat?" Brandon asked.

Nat ignored Brandon and once again invited Andrea to go with her instincts.

Andrea thought about that for a moment, and then put down her burger. She hesitantly picked up the racing form and opened it to that day's card. She stared at it for a while, and then shook her head. "Nothing's coming through, Nat."

"That's okay. Don't rush it."

Brandon felt as if he were witnessing a disaster in progress. Because of a single lucky event, Nat was putting a lot of pressure on Andrea to do something she had neither the talent nor the training for. Andrea seemed to be uncomfortable trying to give Nat what he wanted. Brandon wanted them both to stop, but he had neither the authority nor the power to back up any demands. He just watched, trying to control his growing alarm.

Andrea smiled briefly.

"She has something," Steve said.

"Take it easy," Nat said. "Let it come."

Andrea set the paper on the counter and let her finger rove across the page. Her finger stopped, and she said, "This is it."

"Are you sure?" Steve asked.

"Coming in loud and clear."

"What is it?" Nat asked.

"Third race. Number five. Unrequited."

Brandon wondered if Andrea was trying to send him a message. First Lovesick, now Unrequited.

Steve said, "I sense a pattern forming here."

"Thanks, Andrea," Nat said.

"Don't thank me yet."

"I have complete confidence in you. If you'll excuse me, I have a phone call to make."

When Nat was gone, Brandon said, "Andrea, I think maybe next time Nat asks to do this you should tell him the radio is broken."

"I'm not forcing Nat to bet on the horse I pick. It wasn't even my idea."

"I know, but maybe we have to save him from himself."

Steve said, "Nat's an adult, Brandon. He's been taking care of himself for a long time."

"Besides," Andrea said, "what if he wins?"

"I wouldn't worry about that, Andrea," Brandon said.

But the fact was that Andrea did win again. Unrequited in the third. "Another lucky guess," Brandon said, not so sure anymore. His skepticism was taking a beating.

"No way, Brandon," Nat said. "Andrea has the Power."

"The Power?" Andrea asked, awed by her own possibilities.

"Absolutely." Nat nodded.

Steve was even more excited than Nat or Andrea. Gambling fascinated him. He was always looking for the main chance. Brandon remembered the previous summer when Steve had promoted the midnight poker games that had almost gotten all of them into such big trouble with the Beverly Hills Beach Club and the police. Steve liked to win, but even more than that, he liked to play.

Now, Steve said, "We must show the proper gratitude and respect for Andrea's talent."

Brandon didn't like the sound of that.

"How?" Andrea asked.

"We have to go to the track," Steve said. "Andrea picks the horses and Nat places the bets."

"No way," Nat said again. "If I place bets for minors, I could get arrested."

Steve tried to convince him that going to the track would be fun and that nobody would ever find out what he'd done. Soon, Andrea and even Brandon were caught up in Steve's enthusiasm.

At last, Nat could hold out no longer. Brandon suspected that Nat was just as eager to test Andrea's Power as Steve was.

Nat said, "All right, all right. You're on. We'll go tomorrow. But don't tell anybody."

"Our secret," Steve assured him.

Despite the fact they were now committed, and the financial investment for each of them would be minimal, Brandon felt uneasy depending on something he considered to be entirely bogus—Andrea's supposed Power.

While Brandon drove her home, Andrea rattled on about how great it would be to go to the track for the first time, and what she would do with all the money if they actually won. Brandon didn't say much, and at last Andrea asked, "Do you think we're doing something wrong?"

"You mean is it against nature or something?"

"Yeah."

"No. I don't think Heaven will smite you. I just think it's stupid."

"Thanks a lot."

"Give me a break, Andrea. I don't think you're stupid. But I don't think you have the Power either."

"Twice in a row, Brandon."

"Luck."

"I find that acceptable till something better comes along."

"I just hope we don't run out."

Like a spring storm Jackie Taylor descended upon Dr. Mel Silver's Century City dental office. Despite Arlene's protests, Mrs. Taylor marched through the reception room and back into the area where Dr. Silver did his work. Arlene followed, still trying to stop her.

Mrs. Taylor found Dr. Silver inclined over the mouth of a man in a dental chair. The man in the chair looked around wildly when Mrs. Taylor entered. She cried, "Mel, I must talk to you." Dr. Silver blinked at her benevolently.

"I'm sorry, Doctor," Arlene said. "I couldn't stop her."

"Arlene, this is Jackie."

"*The* Jackie?" Arlene asked. Chagrined, she left them alone with the man in the chair.

"I must speak with you, Mel," Mrs. Taylor said again.

"Excuse me a minute, Mr. Blechman, will you?"

Mr. Blechman grunted. His mouth was full of stainless dental paraphernalia.

Dr. Silver guided Mrs. Taylor out into the hallway and shut the door. "What's this all about, Jackie? I'm doing a root canal in there."

"This won't take long," Mrs. Taylor said. "It's all over, Mel."

Dr. Silver seemed confused. "What's all over?" he asked.

"Well, for starters, Valentine's Day dinner is off."

"You came all the way over here to cancel a dinner party?"

"I'm not just canceling a dinner party, Mel. I won't let you marry me out of some misguided sense of obligation."

"I don't—"

"I know you don't want any more children, but it's a woman's right to chose, and I've made up my mind to have this baby."

"Baby?"

"You don't have to pretend to be surprised. Kelly told me everything. But don't worry. We don't have to see each other anymore. I won't make any demands on your time or your checkbook."

"Jackie, I—"

"Please don't make this any more difficult than it has to be. I've made up my mind. Good-bye, Mel."

She went away, leaving Dr. Silver staring after her in astonishment. He went back to his patient and said, "What do you know? I'm having a baby."

In a garbled fashion, Mr. Blechman said "congratulations," around all the metal in his mouth.

Dr. Silver said, "Thanks. We'll be done in a minute here, Mister Blechman." He looked toward the door, shook his head, and went back to work.

When Kelly got home from school, she was shocked and frightened to find her mother crying. She was curled up on Kelly's bed hugging an old stuffed panda to her chest.

Kelly got her mother to sit up, and put an arm around her. "What happened, Mom?" Kelly asked.

"I told him about the baby. I told him it was over between us. He just stood there."

Kelly decided she must be talking about Mel. Maybe if he was so insensitive, her mother was better off without him. Kelly said, "I'm so sorry."

Mrs. Taylor drew herself up and shuddered. She stopped crying but continued to sniffle. She said, "Yeah, well. That's life. Time to move on."

Kelly handed her a fresh tissue. She was proud of her mom for being strong, but she wasn't sure her mom was making the best of the situation. Kelly said, "Sure, you can move on, but why put yourself through this if you don't have to? You said yourself more than once that women have the right to choose."

"I guess I've chosen."

Kelly knew that her mom had been considering keeping the baby, and apparently the final decision had been made. Kelly felt as if she were the only rational person left in the world. Despite her feelings of anger against Mel Silver, he and her mom had been tight for a long time, much longer than any of her mom's other recent boyfriends. He must have something to recommend him.

Kelly said, "You mean you're going to give up this great guy, and instead have a baby you don't even want?"

Mrs. Taylor blew her nose mightily and put the stuffed panda aside. She set her hand on Kelly's leg and said, "There's a lot more to having an abortion than just the medical procedure."

Kelly was so stunned by what her mom said that her mind raced for a moment, trying to be sure she was interpreting it correctly. Certainly a woman had a right to chose, but if her mother had already had one abortion, a second one seemed even more serious. Tentatively, Kelly said, "You never told me."

"It's not the kind of thing you share with your ten-year-old daughter."

"You were partying pretty hard during that era, I recall."

"You're right, I'm ashamed to say. I barely knew the father. I had to do it. It was the right thing for me to do at the time."

"Was it awful?" Kelly tried not to imagine the scene.

"Not the procedure itself. But knowing I was doing the right thing didn't make it any easier to do. I promised myself that I'd never make the same mistake again. I promised myself I'd be careful."

"Wow." Kelly knew now that her mom would have to keep the baby. Kelly pondered what this meant, but getting her mind around it all was difficult. Mel Silver, the man who was glad his children were grown, was obviously gone from their lives forever. And she was about to be somebody's big sister.

While she hugged her mother, she wondered what that would be like.

14

A day at the races

WHILE NAT DROVE THEM TO THE RACE TRACK in his old van, Andrea eagerly studied that day's racing form. Brandon didn't understand why someone who had the Power needed to do all that extra work, but he kept his questions to himself. He didn't think they would be appreciated.

"Wow," Andrea exclaimed, "someone hit a pick six and won three hundred twenty thousand dollars. What's a pick six?"

Nat said, "That's when you pick six winners on the same day."

"Wow. Did you ever do that?"

Nat chuckled. "Sure. In my dreams."

By the time they got to the track, the parking lot was almost full. Though he did not consider himself a gambler, Brandon liked to play cards occasionally, and he'd been to Las Vegas a couple of times with his parents. Still, the number of people at the track was a surprise. He'd forgotten that an entire subculture of hard-core gamblers existed.

As they walked to the gate, marveling at the size of the place, Brandon tried to pick out the amateurs from the professionals, the people who were there for the sun and the horses from the people who were there for the money. Most people looked normal; he would have passed them on the street without giving them a second look. A few men were dressed like the touts in *Guys and Dolls*—loud coats, dark shirts and white ties, hats with little fishing lure feathers in them—but even they might have been more caught up in the romance of the track than in the gambling.

Once they'd paid their admissions and gone inside, the place took on a circus atmosphere. It was true that many people studied their racing forms and thrill sheets with a seriousness that made Brandon smile, but he also saw families with kids and couples obviously on a date. Food, trinkets, and books on horse racing were available. In the center of it all was a bronze statue of a horse—probably a legendary big winner.

They passed through a building designed like an old movie theater. It was paneled in dark wood, and losing tickets were thick on the floor. Beyond that, the vista took Brandon's breath away. He stood there with Steve, Andrea, and Nat with his eyeballs hanging out.

Proudly, Nat said, "It's something, isn't it?"

Through the haze, Brandon could see mountains in the distance, but the scale of the park itself was enormous. Brandon was reminded of a baseball or football stadium.

Box seats swept down to bleachers which dropped quickly to a wide open area at the rail. Beyond that was the track itself—a wide avenue of carefully kept brown dirt—and then a large grassy infield where people had picnics and kids climbed on playground equipment. There must have been a tunnel under the track. Brandon turned to look up and up. Above them were the enormous windows of the clubhouse, owner country, and the restaurant. Above all was a roof that reached out over the box seats.

Nat seemed disappointed that Andrea had not yet chosen a horse, but he tried not to rush her. He pointed out that it was early yet, and they had all day.

Trying to look cool, they strolled down to the rail, where in that enormous crowd, Nat ran into somebody he knew. His name was Duke Weatherill, and according to Nat, over the years he'd hit the pick six twice. Nat's friend was dressed conservatively; he looked more like an insurance salesman than a tout. He was warm and friendly and instantly put them at ease.

Nat looked around, and like a conspirator, said to Duke Weatherill, "This little girl has the Power."

"Really?"

Brandon couldn't tell if Duke was really impressed or was just pretending for Nat's sake.

Duke asked Andrea, "Who do you like in this one, honey?"

Brandon cringed at Nat's "little girl" and Duke Weatherill's "honey," and waited for the cold front to roll in. Andrea thought of herself as a liberated '90s kind of woman, and normally she would resent being patronized. But her presence at the track seemed to make everything all right. Maybe the entire situation was too theatrical to be taken seriously. The fact that Duke Weatherill had charm enough for two didn't hurt either.

Andrea just smiled at him and said, "I like the seven horse."

Duke Weatherill considered Andrea's pick. Without even referring to the racing form rolled up in his fist, he said, "Grande Amour. That horse was just shipped in from Argentina. They got a top jock to boot her. Eight to one."

Steve said, "Grande Amour. That means big love." He and Brandon looked at each other and shrugged. Brandon knew what he was thinking. This was another in a series of horses with passion names.

Nat didn't seem to notice. Maybe he was just happy to have a horse to bet on. "Sounds like a bet to me," he said.

"It's nice to have met you," Duke said. "See you at the finish line."

Brandon noticed that he had only been polite, not expressed an opinion about Andrea's selection. When Brandon kept his opinions to himself, it generally meant that he didn't want to start an argument or make somebody feel bad. He was suspicious of Grande Amour's capabilities. But he gave Nat the money he'd promised to bet, after mentally kissing it good-bye.

Brandon stood at the rail with Andrea, Nat, and Steve, thinking that they were all wasting their time. Still, the pageantry of racing was interesting; the man playing the familiar call to the post on his long golden trumpet was a bright touch. With a ringing of a bell, the horses were off.

Brandon had seen so many horse races in movies— including *A Day at the Races*—that the race before him did not seem quite real. The announcer described the action, and the people cheered as the horses churned up the track and threw clods of dirt high into the air.

Much to his surprise, Andrea's horse won for the third time in a row.

Brandon lost his mind for a moment. He and his friends leaped around and hugged each other while they yelled and hooted. Duke Weatherill walked by heading for the cashier's window, and Nat—gloating a little in his delight—went with him.

Losers dropped their tickets or threw them into the air like New Year's confetti. The crowd began to thin out. Brandon, Steve, and Andrea leaned against the rail happily looking out at the scene of their most recent victory. Evidently, like Brandon, Steve and Andrea could not quite believe what was happening. Having the extra money would be nice, but Brandon was more impressed with the fact that Andrea's horse had beat all the other horses to the finish line.

Brandon said, "Tell me the truth, Andrea. How are you doing this?"

Andrea became thoughtful and said, "I don't know. I just get kind of a feeling. Actually, it's getting a little scary." She backed away from the rail, turned, and looked up into the milling crowd.

"Scary?" said Steve. "Are you nuts? You're making us rich."

"I don't know if I can do it again—whatever *it* is."

Though Brandon still did not believe in the Power, he did believe in something called synchronicity—the mysterious connection between two seemingly unrelated events. In this case, the events were Andrea's prediction and the relative speed of a certain horse. He didn't care what it was called as long as it worked.

He said, "Don't analyze it to death, Andrea. Just go with it."

Andrea smiled nervously. When Nat came back to ask her which horse she liked in the next race, she didn't have anything for him.

"That's okay," Nat said. "We'll get the one after. Plenty of races left."

The number of races diminished one by one without Andrea feeling a twinge in her Power. Brandon merely sighed as each race passed. Whatever had possessed Andrea was now gone, and things were back to normal. He'd won a little money—not a fortune, but enough to pay for a nice date some evening. He might even ask Andrea.

Nat was frustrated, but he tried to remain calm. Steve, however, was a fount of sarcasm. He eventually declared that he suspected Andrea was holding back on purpose, though he could not explain what that purpose might be.

After a while they all just stood and watched without enthusiasm when the horses ran.

There was still time to bet on the last race, though Brandon didn't think much about it, when Andrea said, "I don't believe it." She was staring at her racing form.

"What?" Brandon, Steve, and Nat asked together.

Excitedly, Andrea told them she'd found a horse in the last race called Cupid's Wing.

"Cupid's Wing?" Steve asked. "That's our horse? You're sure?"

"I guess so."

Andrea did not sound as confident as she had earlier. Still, she'd been right every time she'd actually chosen a horse, and Brandon was willing to give her the benefit of the doubt.

Nat studied the racing form for a moment. He said, "Wait a minute, you guys. This horse is an eighty to one shot. She hasn't even come close in her last six races. I think she's in way over her head." He peered at Andrea and asked her if she was sure.

Andrea worked her mouth in and out. Brandon told himself that she was suffering from some kind of neurotic fear of success.

Andrea said, "I think so," which was not the solid recommendation she had been famous for, but Nat took it at face value. He went to place their bet.

When that was settled, Brandon, Steve, and Andrea noticed how hungry they were. Brandon and Steve went to get some hot dogs, leaving Andrea alone with her ambivalence. She knew that she never had any Power. What she had was dumb luck, and that could run out anytime. Cupid's Wing seemed like such a long shot, she suspected she had run out of dumb luck already. She would feel terrible if her friends lost all their winnings because of her.

Somebody said, "Which horse does Lady Luck pick in the next race?"

Andrea found Duke Weatherill standing next to her, staring at her inquisitively. She smiled and said, "I like Cupid's Wing."

"She *could* win, I suppose," Duke said.

"What do you mean?" She didn't like the reluctant sound of Duke Weatherill's admission.

Duke claimed that he didn't want to jinx whatever she was doing, so it was only with difficulty that Andrea was able to pry some advice out of him. She listened with increasing alarm. According to Duke,

Cupid's Wing was a sucker bet. Like Nat, Duke thought Cupid's Wing was out of her class. The only reason she was even in this race was because the owner hoped somebody would buy her.

"You're saying there's no way Cupid's Wing can win this race."

Duke smiled and said, "Anything can happen, honey, but I have to tell you, that nag is one leg short of a set."

Andrea thanked him and ran off to find Nat before he did something they would all be sorry for.

Nat was already in line at the betting window when she caught up with him. He was determined to bet on Cupid's Wing despite her assurance that she and her Power had been wrong. It was only when she told him about her discussion with Duke Weatherill that Nat seemed to waver.

Andrea said, "Duke knows what he's talking about and I'm just making stupid guesses. He said to bet on Follow Me Home."

"According to the tote board, Follow Me Home is five to one. Now three to one. Cupid's Wing is sixty to one."

"If we lose, it doesn't matter what the odds are, does it, Nat?"

Nat considered that until it was his turn at the window. Andrea watched him make his bet while she waited nervously in the center of the long hall. He came away putting tickets into his pocket.

"Which horse did you bet on?" she asked anxiously.

Unaccountably, Nat seemed very calm now. He

just smiled confidently, said, "Ask me after the race," and strolled outside to the track.

This final test of the "thin air" method of handicapping was maddening. Andrea didn't even know which horse to cheer for. Despondently, she followed Nat.

15

Follow your heart

WHEN BRANDON AND STEVE RETURNED TO THE rail with hands full of hot dogs, they were surprised that Andrea was not there. While they munched on the dogs they had singled out as their own, they joked about the possibility that Andrea was in the barn talking to the horses, finding out which of them they had chosen among themselves to win the next race.

By the time Nat and Andrea showed up, the race was about to begin. Brandon and Steve had time only to distribute the hot dogs before the starting bell sounded.

Right from the beginning, things did not go well for Cupid's Wing, but Brandon and Steve continued to cheer for her until it was impossible that she would finish any way but dead last.

Brandon was shocked. Andrea's Power had never seemed to be more than a lucky fluke, but apparently he'd believed it more than he imagined for the loss surprised him mightily.

He just looked at Andrea mournfully, but the loss had made Steve angry, and he immediately started to complain. He said, "Good one, Andrea. Remind me to leave you home when I go to Las Vegas."

Instead of being surprised at her loss, or even relieved that she no longer had to support a winning streak, Andrea seemed anxious, as if the race were still to be run. Brandon was amazed when she turned to Nat and asked, "Did we win?"

Nat had seemed somber following the race, which made sense if they'd lost, but now he broke into a grin and said, "We sure did, Andrea. Follow Me Home at three to one. Dinner is on me."

Brandon and Steve watched with bewilderment while Andrea and Nat hooted and hugged and danced around.

"I don't get it," Steve said. "I thought our horse was Cupid's Wing."

Brandon held up one hand and said, "Excuse me? Nat? Andrea? Excuse me?"

They stopped celebrating, but remained pleased with themselves as they gave their attention to Brandon and Steve.

Nat said, "Andrea here is smarter than all of us put together. She knows the real secret of horse racing and of life, too."

This was all getting a little too metaphysical for Brandon. He asked, "What's that?"

Nat said, "Sometimes you follow your heart, and sometimes you follow your head."

That explanation did not satisfy Brandon, and he could see that it did not satisfy Steve either.

Andrea said, "I figured out another secret to this game, Nat."

"What's that?"

"You should always quit while you're ahead."

"You got that right, sweetie." Nat offered Andrea his arm and they walked off together.

Brandon said, "Maybe they'll explain to us on the way home."

"Maybe," said Steve. "Even if they don't, we can still fall back on another rule of life."

"What's that?"

"Take the money and run."

David knew that great forces were in flux all around him. Still, he was caught unprepared when things came to a head. He got his first clue that something was wrong when Dr. Silver came down to breakfast and wandered around the kitchen in a morose funk. Dr. Silver got a coffee mug and stood in front of the coffee maker for a long time, contemplating it as if it were full of wisdom instead of coffee.

"You okay, Dad?"

"Fine, fine." He poured himself some coffee and sat down across from David.

David watched him with trepidation. Something had obviously gone wrong, and it probably had to do with Jackie Taylor's baby. David had been dreading the inevitable confrontation when the whole situation at last blew up in their faces.

"Any little thing you'd like to discuss with me, Dad?"

Dr. Silver shook his head for a long time, and then he said, "Maybe you can explain how I managed to shoot myself in the foot."

"Beats me, Dad. What happened?"

"Jackie walked into my office yesterday and broke up with me." He sniffed his coffee delicately, but did not drink any of it.

David was astonished. He didn't think a baby could cause this much trouble. He said, "She did? Why?"

"David, I'm embarrassed to tell you this, but Jackie is pregnant."

"I already knew that."

"You did?" Dr. Silver asked with surprise. "How?"

David did not care to mention Donna's name in this connection. Hoping to change the subject slightly, he said, "It's kind of complicated. I don't understand why the baby made Jackie break up with you."

Fortunately, Dr. Silver was in no mood to pursue the source of David's knowledge. He said,

"Somehow Jackie got the idea that the only reason I want to marry her is because she's pregnant. Or did you already know that, too?"

David didn't already know it, but he had no difficulty tracing his disclosure of the impending proposal from Donna to Kelly and then to Jackie. Jackie was certainly capable of drawing the wrong conclusion—overreacting to something that had never happened. Undoubtedly, Donna would be very apologetic about her part in all this. The information would just have slipped out. But where Jackie had heard the news did not matter now. Describing each link in the chain would not change how she felt. The only thing David knew for certain was that not counting his father's part in actually making the baby, he was entirely innocent.

David said, "I'm sorry, Dad."

"Not your fault."

"So, what are you going to do?"

"If all else fails, I'll do what men have been doing for centuries. I'll beg."

David nodded, and thought about all the times he'd begged himself. Obviously, life did not get simpler after high school.

Soon, Dr. Silver poured his untouched coffee into the sink and said, "I'm going out for a while."

They both knew his destination. It did not need to be said. "Good luck, Dad."

David was going bicycle riding with Donna that afternoon, but he had time to wait around the house for his dad to return. The poor guy might need somebody to talk to. David went upstairs to see if he could make any progress on the song he was writing.

The song was finished, and David had started another when he heard the kitchen door slam. A few minutes later, slow steps came up the stairs and Dr. Silver stood in the open doorway of David's room.

If anything, Dr. Silver looked even more discouraged than he had when he'd left.

David said, "How'd it go, Dad?"

"She wouldn't even listen to me. Kelly would listen, but she was angry and sarcastic. Evidently that baby is a real sore point with the Taylor women."

"You should have been more careful."

Dr. Silver said, "Yeah," and sighed. "I guess I'll just have to learn to live with it. Time heals all wounds." David got the impression that this wound would take quite a while to heal.

Eventually Dr. Silver went to his office, leaving David alone in the house again. It was very quiet, and the occasional sounds of traffic seemed very far away. He turned on some music, but could find nothing depressing enough to fit his mood. Something had to be done. His dad had tried and failed, so maybe it was David's turn now. He had the comfort of knowing he couldn't make things any worse.

He rode to Donna's house on his bicycle. As usual, she looked terrific, having chosen to wear on this occasion brightly colored spandex.

They rode together over the clean white streets of Beverly Hills. The air was warm for February, and they were both soon sweating. David knew what he had to do, but was fearful of trying. At last, Donna said, "I feel as if I'm riding by myself, David. You haven't said anything for five miles."

David admitted he had a lot on his mind, and then Donna admitted that the entire predicament was her fault, and then David assured her that the facts of the case would have come out eventually whether Donna had said anything or not. There was no way to know for sure this was true, of course, but it made David feel better to think so, and it seemed to make Donna feel better, too.

They were both quiet for a long time. Streets that seemed flat when riding in an automobile had a definite slope when riding a bicycle. Sweating pleased David: maybe he was working off some of his tension; maybe the chemicals generated by his exercising body would make him smarter or more creative. He'd heard that such things actually happened.

When Donna suggested he talk to Jackie, the very action he'd been considering himself, David knew it was the right thing to do. Donna sometimes made mistakes because of her enthusiasm, but if she took the time to consider, her answers were generally as useful as anybody else's. She sometimes made astonishing intuitive leaps.

David accompanied Donna home, and then rode over to the Taylor house. He stood at the curb for a long time, working up his nerve before he walked to the door and rang the bell.

Kelly answered the door, and when she saw him she almost slammed it in his face. Only the intervention of Jackie caused her to open the door wider and grudgingly allow him in.

Jackie led David into the living room, as if this were a real visit and not a showdown. Jackie didn't appear to be any happier than his father. Her eyes were red as if she'd been crying, and if a smile came, it went away quickly. Her voice was tired with long-suffering patience, which irritated David. As far as he could tell, it was his father who had suffered most. Jackie had brought this onto herself by jumping to conclusions.

Jackie said, "I know this is difficult for you, David, but believe me, I'm not trying to hurt either you or your father."

"But you are hurting him," David said angrily. "He doesn't understand why you're doing this, and neither do I."

"Your father doesn't want any more children, and I'm not going to second-guess his decision. I don't want him to marry me just because he thinks he has to." She pulled a tissue from a box and loudly blew her nose.

Jackie's self-righteousness made talking to her easier because it disgusted him a little. David said, "My dad wanted to marry you way before he knew you were pregnant."

"David, please—"

"You have to believe me."

David perceived the first crack in Jackie's

assurance when she asked, "You didn't tell him I was pregnant?"

"No." He had to tell the entire story again—what Donna had told him and what he'd told Donna.

Jackie asked, "Well, if you didn't tell him I was pregnant, then who did?"

"You did," David said. "At the office the day you broke up with him."

"Oh."

David could see that he'd made the right impression. He stood up, thanked Jackie for her time and let himself out. Further discussion would only muddy up the waters again. What Jackie Taylor needed at the moment was time to grasp the new facts and work out what to do. David suspected that Jackie loved his dad as much as he loved her. She would do the right thing. If not, maybe she wasn't the right woman for his father after all.

Whereas before, Jackie Taylor had descended upon Dr. Mel Silver's dental practice like a force of outraged nature, she now touched down as lightly as a feather. She politely requested of Arlene a moment of Dr. Silver's valuable time. Arlene gazed upon Mrs. Taylor suspiciously for a moment, and then went to speak with her boss. She came back a moment later and told Mrs. Taylor that Dr. Silver was in room three.

Mrs. Taylor entered room three demurely and apologized for the way she'd acted on the previous visit. Dr. Silver looked up from the instruments he'd been organizing on a tray. Surprised but pleased by Jackie's presence, he quickly forgave her.

Mrs. Taylor said, "I talked to David, Mel."

"That's nice," Dr. Silver said, baffled.

"Is it true that you wanted to marry me before you knew I was pregnant?"

"Yes," Dr. Silver cried. "That's what I kept trying to tell you."

"I guess I really made a fool of myself."

"Your passion is one of the things I like about you."

Mrs. Taylor smiled and looked down. Dr. Silver fiddled with his dental instruments.

She said, "But what about the baby? You said you didn't want any more children."

"I didn't say I didn't want any more. I said that I was glad Kelly and David were nearly grown. But I like babies. And a new one is coming. It will need us. Both of us."

"Oh, Mel," Mrs. Taylor said and laid a hand on his arm.

He said, "I was going to wait till this evening, but what the hell?" He got down on one knee and held up a small velvet box he found in the pocket of his white smock. "I want to spend the rest of my life with you and our child. Marry me, Jackie."

Mrs. Taylor took the ring and began to cry. "Yes, Mel. Oh, yes." They embraced.

* * *

In the mail that day, Kelly Taylor got a Valentine's card from Steve Sanders. Which was just as well because Kelly had sent one to him. Neither card was exactly romantic, having obviously been found in the "Humorous" section of the card store. Although she'd been involved in it for some years, Kelly did not understand her relationship with Steve. When he'd gone to Albuquerque the previous Christmas to search for his real mother, she'd missed him a lot and was glad when he'd come back. But sometimes she couldn't stand being around him. She loved him but they weren't friends. Ah, sweet mystery of life.

Somehow, David Silver had actually fixed things between his dad and her mom, and the Valentine's Day dinner was on again. Kelly had made up with Donna, and Donna would be there, too, which would be nice. Donna was one of her best friends.

Mel, Donna, and David arrived, and Kelly welcomed them more cordially than she had the previous time. Mel brought along a few bottles of sparkling cider, and he got Jackie out of the kitchen to make a toast that brought tears to everybody's eyes. "To you, Jackie," he said, "and to babies born of love."

In her own mind, Kelly admitted that she'd been wrong about Mel Silver—maybe wrong about the whole Silver family. They had weathered one of Jackie's three-day blows, and come through it smiling. These were not ordinary men.

Donna said, "Gee, Kel, if Jackie and Mel are getting married, I guess that makes you and David sister and brother."

The thought seemed to amuse Jackie and Mel, but Kelly found the idea repulsive. Evidently, this was the first David had thought about their relationship, too. He meditated on Kelly, not unfriendly, but considering. Mel had toasted new beginnings. Kelly was just starting to realize what that meant.

Brenda could not tell if Dylan was hanging around the Walsh kitchen because he had nothing better to do, or because he wanted to further tease her about where they were going for Valentine's Day. Of course, today was Valentine's Day, and if he intended to make his move that evening he could not maintain the mystery much longer. She was frustrated that she could not guess the answer.

"How long are you going to keep this up?" she asked.

"Till this evening."

"Give me another clue." Brenda was certain that given the right clue, she could salvage her honor and figure out the puzzle before Dylan gave her the solution.

"Okay. You have to be at least seventeen to do what we're going to do tonight."

Brenda wondered for a moment whether Dylan was going to take her to see an X-rated movie, but she knew that would not be like him. He was more likely to drag her off to some ancient black-and-white romantic comedy. Besides an X-rated movie did not fit any of the other clues.

While Brenda continued to ponder, her parents came downstairs dressed for the evening. Her father was wearing business attire, but her mom looked terrific in one of the formal dresses she did not get the opportunity to wear very often. Brenda was both pleased and a little embarrassed that on her cheeks she wore some of the Apricot Temptation blusher she'd purchased under duress when Brenda had worked at Tracy Ross.

Dylan was very complimentary, but that did not distract Mr. Walsh from asking, "So, what are your plans for the evening?"

"Ask Dylan. I don't even know where we're going," Brenda said.

Mr. Walsh asked, "Your plans don't involved anything, uh, dangerous, or, you know, risqué?"

"Oh, Dad," Brenda said, horrified by his lack of trust.

"Don't worry, sir," Dylan said. "We'll be well taken care of in a public place."

Another clue, Brenda thought triumphantly. It was something only adults could do, lying down, and in a public place. It was warm, red, and close to her heart. She shook her head. This was worse than algebra.

She said, "At least tell me what to wear. Are we going on a hike or to a museum?"

"Wear whatever you want, Bren, but I'd advise you to wear short sleeves."

What did short sleeves have to do with Valentine's Day?

Dylan promised to pick her up at seven, and then left without commenting further. Brenda was not angry, exactly, but she was definitely miffed enough to wear long sleeves. However, while she went through her closet looking for something appropriate to wear on a mystery date, she decided to make it easy on herself. Dylan would certainly not have advised short sleeves unless they were necessary.

She had sorted through almost her entire closet before she decided to wear clothes a little fancier than what she might wear to school, but not so fancy that she had to be afraid of doing terminal damage to them if Dylan's idea of Valentine's Day romance turned out to be more rustic than he'd suggested. And she wore short sleeves.

Dylan showed up at seven dressed in a sport coat and slacks. About the same level of fancy Brenda herself was dressed at, she saw with some relief. He offered her flowers and a big red heart filled with chocolates.

She melted into his arms, but he would not allow them to kiss for long. "We'll be late for the play."

"Play?" Brenda asked. Laying down? Over seventeen? Huh?

"It's called *Love Letters*, and it's about a man and a woman who had a love so pure and honest that it blossomed over the years despite the fact they never met, only wrote letters."

"Dylan, that's beautiful. But what has that got to do with all your clues?"

"Nothing. The clues have to do with the place we're going first."

And still, Dylan would not tell her where they were going. They got into his Porsche and set off. The longer Dylan drove, the more Brenda recognized the route. With surprise, Brenda said, "You can't be taking us to school."

"I can and I am."

"This isn't funny, Dylan. Especially after keeping me in suspense for weeks."

"Give me a chance here, Bren. I promise you won't be disappointed."

Brenda trusted Dylan, but she could not help feeling disappointed and betrayed. She tried to remain hopeful that Dylan would somehow redeem himself, but it was an effort. How romantic could *anything* be if they did it at school?

Brenda was surprised at the number of cars in the student parking lot. Dylan led her around to the auditorium. Over the door was a banner that said RED CROSS BLOOD DRIVE. Under that it said, "Save a life with a gift from your heart."

Brenda said, "I have to admit it's different." All she could think about was needles. She hated needles.

"But I was straight with you all the way: you have to be seventeen, you do it lying down in a public place, and blood is red, warm, and close to your heart."

"It's probably a good thing you didn't tell me. I might not have come."

"It's really no big a deal. You'll see."

Through the open door, Brenda saw nurses moving quietly among people lying on narrow cots. Nobody seemed to be in pain. Maybe it wasn't such a big deal.

Dylan put his arm around her and said, "I've been waiting a long time to do this. I was in a bad car accident when I was a kid and I lost a lot of blood." He touched his right eyebrow where a scar ran nearly its entire length. Brenda had often wondered how he'd come by that scar. She'd always supposed it had happened in some surfing accident.

"I can't thank the people who gave the blood that saved my life, but I can save another life with *my* blood. Our blood. Giving somebody back his or her life was the most romantic thing I could think of for us to do together."

"That's why you wanted to do it on Valentine's Day."

"Partly. Also, the accident happened on Valentine's Day."

Brenda nodded. Needle or no needle, she wanted to do this with Dylan, not only because it was romantic, but because it was noble, and the right thing to do. She could not help being a little scared, but she'd overcome her fears before. She'd revealed herself in a drama class. She'd learned to drive. Giving blood would be no worse.

She and Dylan did the paperwork and soon were lying side by side. The needle in her arm felt strange, but after a single prick, it did not hurt much. She gripped Dylan's free hand tightly with her own. This was a Valentine's Day she would never forget.

Go back to the beginning...
See the 90 minutes that started it all!

THE BEVERLY HILLS, 90210 HOME VIDEO
available in video stores everywhere January 1992.

Don't Miss An Issue!